Clarice Bean
Think Like an Elf

CANDLEWICK PRESS

Lauren Child

The Twelve Days of Christmas

The Beginning of Things

ONE THING WE ALL AGREE ON IN OUR
house is that we like looking forward
to Christmas.

My favorite song for this time of the year is
"The Twelve Days of Christmas."
I'm not sure exactly what it is about.
I used to think it was Christmas shopping,
but Betty Moody says it has to do with
the twelve days AFTER Christmas.

But why would someone give you
ALL those presents when it is all OVER?

And why would they give you
so many BIRDS?

It might be about
the holiday sales,
but Betty says they
DIDN'T have sales
in the
olden days.

When the Christmas
seaon begins, I sing "The
Twelve Days of Christmas"
ALL THE TIME,
but I tend not to know
what comes AFTER
the seven swans
are swimming.

7

Speaking of seven, we also have seven in our family. Which is:

my mom and my dad;

my older brother, Kurt;

my older sister, Marcie;

Me, Clarice Bean;

my grandad, who is an *actual* live-in older relative;

and my younger brother, Minal Cricket.

If we were like those families in the books, we would look like THIS,

all nicely sitting down, listening to each other
in a smiling way—like you see
on Christmas cards.

But usually, actually, we look more like THIS . . .

which is t**a**l**k**i**n**g
or
NOT t**a**l**k**i**n**g
all at the same time
from different
rooms.

I live on Navarino Street,
number 7, and I know LOTS
of the people on our road.
At Christmastime there is
more helloing
and this is because of the
Christmas spirit.

Christmas cannot be Christmas
without the Christmas spirit,
so it is IMPORTANT to
keep an eye on it and
NOT let it float away.

ONE

Christmas Is Coming, the Goose Is Getting Fat

YOU CAN TELL WHEN IT'S GETTING TO BE Christmas because Mom gets out the Christmas-elf dish towels. We have three of them although we used to have four. Granny sent them to us—they are from New York and along the bottom they say "Think Like Elves" in embroidery.

We have special Christmas water glasses too, which have reindeers on the sides. They are very old. No one must break them because they are heirlooms of the family and very much the spirit of Christmas.

Every year Dad says, "We drank from these glasses when I was a SMALL child and NOT one of them has ever been dropped."

This makes me very actually nervous.

There are only six so not quite enough to go around, but Grandad says he's happy with a less valuable water glass, as he suffers from the collywobbles, which basically means he is liable to drop a glass at any moment.

The other thing which usually happens is that we all bake gingerbread cookies, which are decorated with icing. They are sort of chewy and NOT necessarily that nice unless you are in the mood. But I don't mind because it is another sign that

Christmas
is
coming.

Something you may also notice is that there is more mail: electric bills with holly printed on the envelope, and cards from people who you can't remember who they are.

If I come downstairs to hear Mom saying,
"Who are Beryl and Terrance?"

and Dad saying,
"I haven't got a clue,"

then
I know
that

Christmas

has

begun.

Actually we never know who
Beryl and Terrance are.

I'm beginning to wonder if
they even know us.

Also we don't know who

J and P and W (Farrell) are,

even though they always write in the card

"Really enjoyed bumping into you
this summer"

or

"W is doing really well with
his clarinet."

Once the Christmas cards begin to arrive,
we arrange them on the kitchen table
and Mom always says,

"It's so lovely to think of all these people
from all these far-off places taking the trouble
to write and send us good cheer."

And then when more arrive, we line them up
along the living-room shelves and then along the
kitchen shelves
and Mom says,
"Look at that—the spirit of Christmas!"

And then when even more come, we crowd them on the window ledges and always a few of them fall into the kitchen sink.

And Mom says, "These cards are a blimming nuisance."

But really there is nowhere else to put them, so it is unavoidable that some end up getting wet.

We used to hang them up on a string across the kitchen, but then one year some of them decided to fall into the stir-fry and they got set on fire, and it could have been much worse if Kurt hadn't thrown a wet dish towel over the wok.

Think Like Elv

My Uncle Ted, who is
a firefighter, told us
our Christmas cards were
a FIRE HAZARD
waiting to happen.
He was right, and we were
lucky **not** to lose more than the
Christmas-elf dish towel.
He said, "You just CANNOT
have Christmas cards
dangling
over open flames.
What were
you thinking?"
Everyone looked sheepish.
So now there is a strict law in
our house about cards—when
too many arrive the ugly
ones get shuffled into
the recycling.

I say, "Mom, you do know you are throwing
people's Christmas spirit in the actual trash can?"
And Mom whispers,
   "Whatever you do, don't tell anyone!"

★ ★ ★

The stores will try to make you believe
Christmas is arriving in October,
but Mom says you must ignore them.
   She says,

      "Could they just let me carve
            my pumpkin, for goodness' sake?
   We haven't even had Halloween yet!"

Some people even send their cards in November,
which is too early, since Christmas can't really
begin until the first of December.
   December first is when you can start opening
      the TINY DOORS on the Advent calendar,
                        and from then on . . .

Christmas is truly coming.

Mind you, this year we don't even have an Advent calendar because Mom decided we would instead have an **Advent candle**, which is basically a candle with numbers on it.

She said,

"It will bring more togetherness
to our home because we will
light it every evening
as a family during supper."

We have to burn it down one notch at a time and then *blow* it out, which is not as interesting as opening a TINY DOOR.

But Granny told me you can use it to make a Christmas wish every time you blow it out, which means twenty-four wishes. I'm going to wish for snow, and if I do it twenty-four times in a row it will probably work even though Dad says the weather people say there's not even a smidge of a chance this year.

Grandad says, "It's going to be *blowing* a gale and it's going to be nothing but gales."
Grandad knows about weather because he was brought up with it.

Most people have those Advent calendars with chocolates, but these have been banned in our house because some people kept eating other people's chocolates and this led to complaints.

Because I'm missing having a real Advent calendar, I've made my own out of paper and I've drawn little pictures for each day. I'm trying to surprise myself by forgetting what is behind the TINY DOORS . . .

So far I have NOT been fooled.

★ ★ ★

Usually we have Christmas at home. I think this is because Mom hates packing and Dad says it is too much effort to get seven people and a dog in a car all at the same time.

This year Mom says she wants a quietish Christmas where nothing much happens. She says, "Let's just be the seven of us."

1
2
3
4
5
6
7
8
9
10
11
12
13
14
15
16
17
18
19
20
21
22
23
24

But some of us prefer things to be more than seven, so I am a bit disappointed by this announcement. You see, I really like the Christmases when LOTS of people come and stay. I thought we ALL did, but it turns out Mom and Dad are feeling exhausted by the thought of it.

I'm not sure how you can be exhausted by a thought, but this seems to be something which happens to you when you get older.

I know this because when Marcie asks, "Why can't everyone come?"

Mom says, "Just thinking about it . . ."

She doesn't even finish her sentence—she just flops down on the chair.

And Dad shakes his head and says, "Exactly."

And Mom says, "I feel exhausted already."

Kurt says, "But it's no fun if everyone isn't here."

Everyone is surprised by this because Kurt normally doesn't bother with fun. He just spends all his time in his room with headphones on.

Marcie says, "It will be totally BORING if it's only us."

Minal says, "Yes, let's have everyone!"

Dad says, "If you four are prepared to do all the shopping and all the cooking, then fine—ask as many people as you want."

I say,
"Thanks, we will."

Marcie and Kurt stomp off to their rooms,
and Minal says,

"Don't look at me—I'm standing on my head."

Which, by the way, he is NOT.

My brother CAN'T do headstands.

I say, "OK, I will do everything."

Dad says, "I'll write you a shopping list."

Mom says, "The recipe books are on the shelf
next to the fridge."

Dad says, "How many people are you thinking of inviting?"

I say, "Twelve."

I say twelve because I've got the song "The Twelve Days of Christmas" stuck in my brain. It's like there are people singing it inside my actual head and I can't stop them.

Mom says, "So twelve plus the seven of us makes nineteen in all. How many potatoes will you need to cook, I wonder?"

Dad says, "At least four per person—are you inviting Uncle Ted?"

I say, "Of course—he is the MAIN one."

Dad says, "Well, Ted always eats extra, and it's nice to have some left over for Boxing Day . . . so better make it six each plus a few for the pot."

I can't even work out what 19 x 6 is— let alone how much a few for the pot comes to. I am busy trying to do the times-ing but then Dad says,

"One hundred and fourteen potatoes plus about six more!"

I say, "How am I going to peel
   one hundred and fourteen potatoes
        plus six more?"
Mom says, "You'll just have to get up early."
Dad says, "I suggest five a.m."
I'm not really an early rising sort of person,
and I go up to my room feeling strangely tired.
I'm beginning to understand how a thought can
actually wear you out, since just thinking about
counting out one hundred and fourteen plus six
potatoes has made me need to lie down.

If I'm this tired just thinking about peeling
potatoes, then how will I feel after I have actually
done them? I expect I won't have the energy to
talk or cook a turkey or maybe even to watch TV.
I decide it's useless to try to make Christmas more
than seven.

   Slowly I am feeling the Christmas spirit

        evaporating

             out   of

                  me.

TWO

Goodwill to All Peoplekind

IN THE MIDDLE OF THE NIGHT AT 5 A.M., while I am still awake worrying about the evaporating Christmas spirit, I begin to see how it is more important than ever to spread goodwill to all peoplekind, since we won't now be peeling potatoes for them.

If we are not going to be sharing our Christmas spirit on the actual day of Christmas, then at least I can put some into mailboxes.

I'm going to need a LOT more cards than usual. I always make my own cards. Mom says it is more personal this way and "so much better than just going to the store and buying them off the rack." This is very easy for her to say because she is NOT the one working herself down to the fingers.

Normally I tend to leave the making to the last minute because there is so much else to do. This can have a benefit because you can see who sent you a card, and you can see who DIDN'T, which means you don't have to find yourself sending cards to people who don't bother sending one to you. Although when I explained this to Mom, she said that strictly speaking this is NOT in the Christmas spirit.

She told me, "You should mail cards to anyone and everyone—it doesn't matter if you don't get one back."

This must be what Beryl and Terrance have decided, because we never send them one back— we can't. We don't know their address! I have decided to be influenced by Beryl and Terrance, and I'm going to make cards for ALL the neighbors on our street even if I don't know them. I will also send one to the corner store, one to the post-office-convenient store, one to the vegetarian organic shop which is called Eggplant, and maybe also the vet because Dad says we need to keep on their good side.

Mom says generosity can have a good effect on bad relationships, so I will also make cards for people who don't like me.

This means **Mrs. Stampney.**

Mrs. Stampney lives next door and will not return a Frisbee if it lands in her yard.

I prefer to make my
Christmas cards
on the floor of my
bedroom—

though nowadays I steer clear
of the carpet
because of a marker incident.

I used to like drawing a shape in glue and
pouring glitter all over it—glitter makes
everything instantly better than it was.

34

But my
brother Kurt
says

glitter is a **HAZARD** to fish.

He says it gets into the oceans and causes
problems and you WOULDN'T believe
how many fish are eating glitter these days.

You wouldn't think something so SMALL could cause problems to something so big, i.e., the sea. But Kurt is an environmentalist and he knows about these things.

So now I'm trying to come up with other ways of creating the Christmas effect without making fish eat glitter.

The question is I need a good idea. I've been STRETCHING my brain to think how I can make cards out of something that causes less trouble in the ocean. It needs to be something which doesn't cost any money, so it has to be something I've already got.

Minal says, "Why don't you use macaroni?"

That's his answer to EVERYTHING and he has gotten everyone to buy tons of it, and now Mom says he's going to have to make a LOT more jewelry or we'll never get through it.

I say, "I'm not going to stick dried-up food on my cards, thank you very much."

Kurt says, "Why don't you recycle stuff instead of using the planet's valuable resources?

It's all going to end up in the trash anyway."

And then suddenly a good idea pops into my head, the way it sometimes does when you are utterly desperate.

I will rescue the Christmas spirit from the trash can where Mom chucked it and

cut up all the ugly cards and turn them into newly reinvented ones.

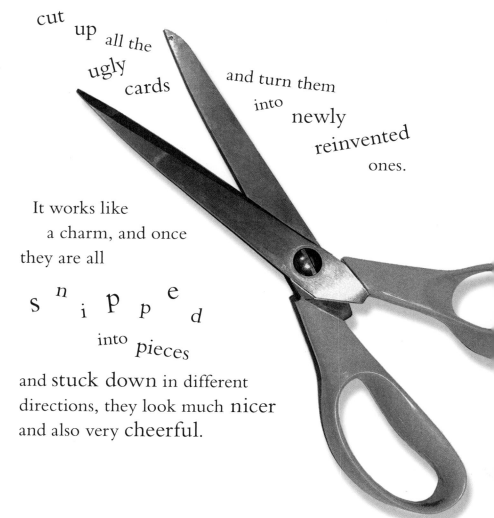

It works like a charm, and once they are all

s n i p p e d into pieces

and stuck down in different directions, they look much nicer and also very cheerful.

Since I am in a making-things frame of mind, I also make Granny a Christmas present, which is a TINY-USEFUL-THINGS BAG—it was meant to be for lavender except I didn't have any.

A good tip to remember when making your gifts is to check that you have the vital ingredients. If not, you must adapt your ambition, which is what I have done.

Once I've finished, I hand it to Mom because she is busy boxing up other presents for Granny, who lives in New York. We have to send them out early because they are traveling a long way so it takes a while. Minal has made Granny his usual macaroni necklace.

Dad says it doesn't matter that it is a repeated gift because Granny wore her last macaroni necklace in a rainstorm and it got ruined.

Mom is really impressed with my TINY-USEFUL-THINGS BAG, and she loves the recycled ugly Christmas cards but whispers, "Just try NOT to mail them back to their original senders."

My recycling has inspired her to do some recycling

of her own and at the same time do a good deed for others and clear out some clutter before Christmas. She is collecting our old sweaters—the ones that have turned into strange shapes and the ones that have holes too big to easily mend without knitting a whole entire sleeve. She is sending them to Mr. Felixstow's knitwear drive. Mr. Felixstow does something with the wool and this turns into money for a good cause.

He wrote to us on a leaflet that came through the door asking for help from strangers. Mom looked it up on the computer and it turns out there's a LOT you can do with old knitted things if you know how.

I wish I knew how because she is giving Mr. Felixstow a couple of my favorite cardigans and I'm sorry to see them go.

Dad says, "I hope you DIDN'T put my Christmas-elf sweater in there."

And Mom says, "Of course not."

But I can tell she is lying because she pretends to sneeze—she always pretends to sneeze when she is telling a WHOPPER.

★ ★ ★

While Mom and I are doing good deeds at home,
Dad and Marcie go off to help Uncle Ted with
his move to a much SMALLER place.

He is now going to be living with his new
girlfriend. She is named JoJo and she has black hair
which is sometimes red
and cut at a SLANT.

She is training to do lighting for the theater
but at the moment is working at the old people's
center being the maintenance person.

Uncle Ted and JoJo need to move into their
apartment in time for Christmas.

Mom says, "They want to spend the day together
in their new home, just the TWO of them."

I don't know why they would want that, but
everyone's being a bit strange this year and has
let the Christmas spirit drift.

Dad and Marcie are gone forever, and they come
back from Uncle Ted's at almost dinnertime. They
are very tired and with LOTS more BOXES of
clutter, more than Mom just got rid of.

Dad says the apartment is very SMALL indeed and Ted and JoJo have had to go MINIMALIST, which means no unneeded items, i.e., all their stuff is moving into our shed.

The good news is that we now have a secondary fridge in the yard.

Marcie says, "Ted and JoJo's apartment looks really cool."

Mom says, "I'm so happy for them."

Marcie says, "Why can't we have a

MINIMALIST house?"

Mom says, "We can—we just need to find someone who is willing to let us put all our clutter in their shed."

Dad says, "I doubt if anyone has a shed big enough for our clutter."

That night we have a simple meal of baked beans, and make-your-own toast.

I ask Mom if I can eat it on my lap while I watch the **RUBY REDFORT** series on TV, but she points to a sign she has written that says:

<u>NO</u> EATING on the C<u>OUCH</u> due to SPILLAGES and crumbs.

Mom says she is also concerned that there might be a possible mouse on the loose. She says, "Cement keeps barking at something,
    and I think it must be a TINY visitor."
Minal says, "He's NOT barking at a mouse—
        he's barking at the FOX."

My brother Minal Cricket is obsessed with foxes since he was given this book about a fox who comes into people's houses when they aren't looking and eats their dinners and finally their Christmas turkey.

Mom says it's the first book that has really caught his imagination.

Minal talks about it non stop, and he thinks it's the most fascinating thing EVER written, though of course it ISN'T.

I understand how you can be so caught up in a book that it almost becomes true. It's like with me and **RUBY REDFORT**. Sometimes I can't help thinking she's real, and I often wish I could go and live in Twinford, which is where Ruby is from. If you don't know who Ruby Redfort is, you should, because she is a book character who is also a kid secret agent, and the stories are really gripping and NOT for drips. There are at least about fifty-two books and all of them get you on the edge of your seat.

Eating at the table instead of on the sofa does remind me that we almost forgot to light the Advent candle—it is very hard to remember this new habit. I make sure I get to blow it out so I can wish for snow, and as soon as I have, I rush to switch the TV on. I am desperate of course to watch because it is the **RUBY REDFORT CHRISTMAS SPECIAL**: PART ONE.

Unfortunately, I've already missed the beginning credits with the FLY LOGO buzzing you into Twinford. The fly is important because this is the symbol for the SECRET AGENCY called **SPECTRUM** where Ruby Redfort works. The episode begins with Mrs. Redfort bringing home a huge Christmas tree—of course it is snowing because in Ruby Redfort's life everything turns out the way it's supposed to. The episode ends on a cliffhanger where Ruby gets told she must jump out of a helicopter and ski to a secret location.

My evening ends with
Mom telling me to
   get off the sofa
   and hop up
      to bed.

THREE

Glad Tidings of Great Joy

ONE OF THE SECOND FIRST THINGS
you need to do when you are getting ready for
Christmas is make a list of all the things you
will need to buy for your dearest ones and your
younger brother. Then you need to look in your
piggy bank—mine is a toadstool—and discover
that you are probably going to have to hand-make
almost all your gifts because the price of things
is NOT covered by your pocket money.
Especially when you are hoping to spend more
than you actually have on a present for your
friend Betty Moody.

The thing I want to buy her is this: **THE RUBY REDFORT FLY READER BOOK LIGHT**. The light is a fly attached to a bendy thing and it clips on to your book when you want to read in the dark and it's mail-order only.

I need to order it soon or it WON'T arrive in time.

But it is utterly OUT of my price range.

It's easy to shop for Betty Moody, but it is hard to think of things that everyone else might like. Especially things that you can actually make for not too much money.

In the end I think it will come down to fudge.

These are the people on my list:

Mom: fudge
Dad: fudge
Kurt: fudge
Marcie: fudge
Grandad: fudge
Minal: fudge
Uncle Ted: fudge
Betty Moody: Ruby Redfort Fly Light
Karl Wrenbury: fudge
Granny: tiny-useful-things bag

I have also made a list of the things I'd like for Christmas, and this is it:

A piano

Piano music

A pair of roller skates

A Ruby Redfort long-distance secret-agent walkie-talkie

A fish tank

Some fish

Some fish food

Snow

I have added snow because I don't know if the Advent candle is up to it—the granting wishes, I mean. I'm not sure if this is an up-the-chimney for Santa list or a list for Mom and Dad. We have always sent our lists up the chimney even though you can also send them in the mail. Sometimes I think that maybe my mom and dad have taken over from Santa. I've asked about this, but they always say it ISN'T true. But I'm puzzled by why Santa and my mom and dad would use the same wrapping paper. I mean, I'm not sure why Santa would bother to get his wrapping paper from the post-office-convenient store on Park Road if he really does live all the way at the North Pole.

Dad says, "He probably likes their selection, and the prices aren't bad."

But I would have thought Santa would have his own convenient store. I'm certain it would be more convenient to buy wrapping paper from somewhere near his actual workshop.

I'm still trying to make a decision about this problem when Mom calls out that Betty is on the phone.

As you know, Betty Moody is my best friend. She is in my class—we always sit together. Betty asks if I'd like to come over and have lunch at her house. Which I would because I like going over to the Moodys'. Betty calls her mom and dad by their first names, and if anyone ever calls them Mr. and Mrs. Moody they always say, "Call me Cecil," or "Call me Mol." They are very friendly people.

Because I don't want to waste any time not being at Betty's, I start stuffing cards into their envelopes. This is tricky because I didn't think of what size the envelopes would be when I made the cards, so it is a tight squeeze and some folding.

I want to deliver my neighborhood cards on the way to the Moodys' as this is sensible doubling-up, which is known as multitasking. It is very wise to multitask at Christmas because there is SO much to do.

Mom says, "Goodness me, you have certainly made a LOT of cards. Who are they all for?"

I explain that most of them are for the people on our street.

I say, "The ones I don't know I have just written on the envelope, 'for the occupant,' because I have seen this done with some of our letters from the government and the junk mail people do it too."

Dad says, "This might look a bit impersonal."

I can see what he means. Mom agrees.

She says, "It's NOT very Christmassy."

Marcie says, 'They'll probably put it in the trash."

So we quickly cross this out and instead I add:

To my neighbors

Dad says, "Much more friendly!"

It's true—this is much more in the style of Christmas.

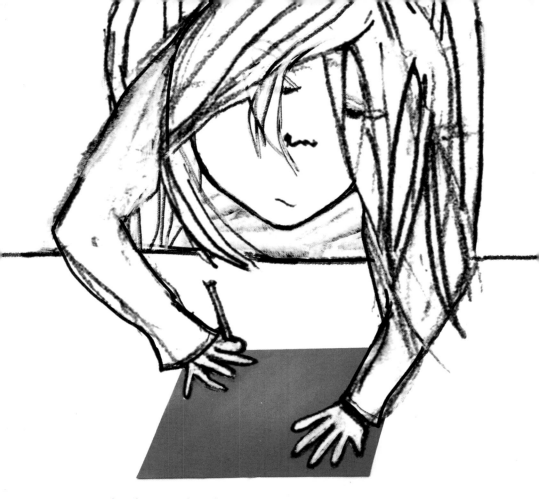

Inside the cards I have written:

Dear neighbor,
Wishing you glad tidings of joy from
a well-wisher in your neighborhood.
Clarice Bean

I deliver all my neighbor cards on the way to Betty's house. All except for ONE, where there is a dog parked on the other side of the gate who looks a bit interested in eating my card or my sleeve.

And that would mean ANOTHER donation for Mr. Felixstow.

While I am walking, I think
about my Santa list and I can't
help wondering HOW he is going to
fit a piano in a stocking.

It doesn't take long to get to the Moodys' house because they are more or less around the corner, just five or so streets away.

The Moodys' house is upside down,* the same as Ruby Redfort's, but it doesn't have a laundry chute.

When I get there, I ring the doorbell, which makes a pipe-ish sound because it is unusual and not the boring kind of doorbell, and possibly from the Far East. Betty answers in socks.

No shoes are worn in the Moodys' home. We go upstairs to the kitchen, and call-me-Cecil says, "Hello, Clarice Bean.

You are just in time for lunch!"

Call-me-Mol says,

"We are having macrobiotic soup."

I do not know if this is a vegetable or a flavor, but it sounds interesting to me.

The Moodys always eat things that you've never heard of.

* An upside-down house is one where the bedrooms are on the first floor and the kitchen and living room are above.

Mol says, "Clarice, do you like daikon, pickled?"
And I don't know because I have no idea what
it is even when it ISN'T pickled.
But I say yes, because it's important
to expand what you eat.

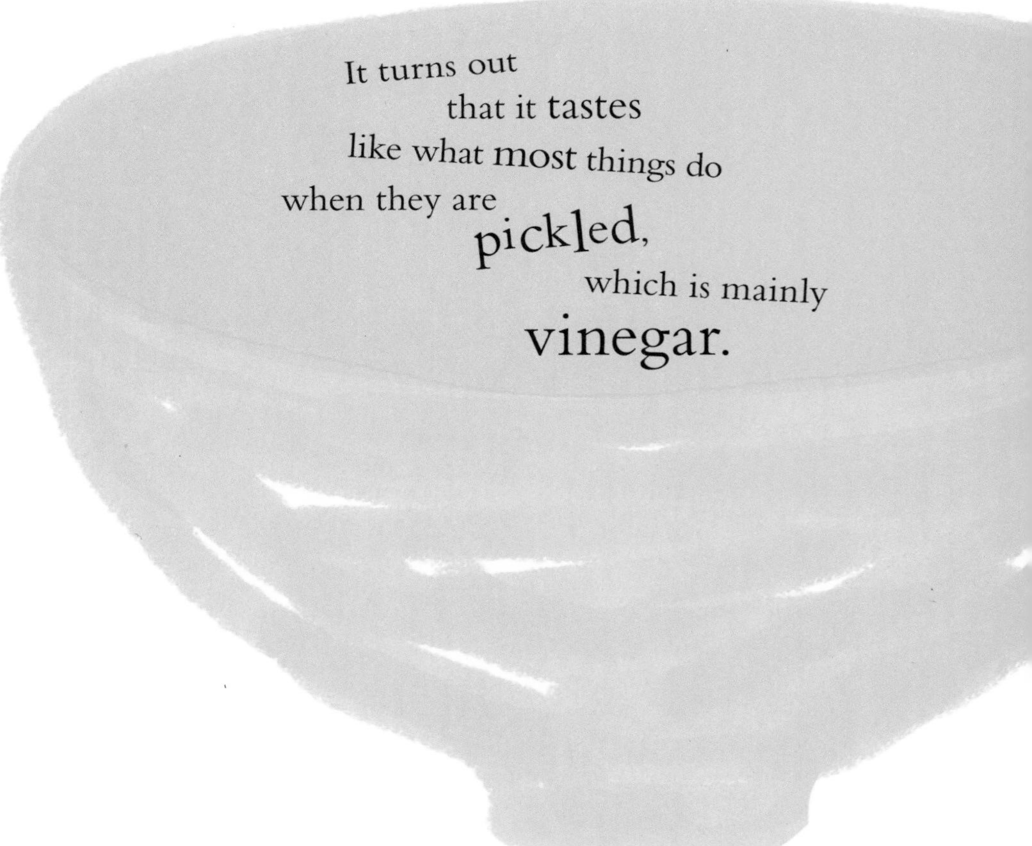

It turns out
that it tastes
like what most things do
when they are
pickled,
which is mainly
vinegar.

The Moodys want Betty to see Japan, so they are going there for Christmas.

I wish my mom and dad wanted me to see Japan. The Moodys are traveling there along with Betty's much older brother, Zack, to visit his girlfriend and her family, who are, in fact, Japanese.

It is a shame for me because it means I will not see Betty for most of the Christmas break.

Usually we even see each other on the actual Christmas Day, but this year we will be sadly separated and not together. However, on the plus side, Betty said she will bring me back some of those big-toe socks that you can wear with flip-flops.

These kinds of socks are hard to find here but not in Japan. I have always wanted some.

Mol says, "It will be a different sort of Christmas." Which is true because Betty won't even arrive in Japan until Christmas Day in the morning, so Christmas for her will start by NOT being anywhere at all.

Mol says,
"This will be interesting,"

and Betty says,
"And also fun."

And I say how I couldn't agree more because the Moodys will be surrounded by hundreds of traveling people and Christmas is all about being with people. And then I tell Mol how my mom and dad have reduced Christmas to seven and how disappointed I feel, "Because that is almost hardly anyone! It makes me feel like Christmas has utterly fallen apart before it has started."

Mol looks out the window like she is trying to see something, but I think it's in her head, the something she's trying to find. And then she says,

"As Marilyn Monroe
once said, 'Sometimes
good things fall apart
    so better things
        can fall together.'"

Marilyn Monroe is a famous movie
star from the olden days, and me and
Grandad like watching her movies when
it's a damp afternoon. Usually they're
in black and white.

Mol says,
    "So my advice would be,
        focus on what's good,
    and Christmas may well
        surprise you."

Mol has a habit of saying things in a way that makes you think she knows something you don't know, so when she says this I feel strangely better. But of course there's another problem.

I say, "That's the other problem. I'm trying to focus on making things good, but I'm a bit stuck with my presents because it turns out my toadstool doesn't have that much money in it, so I'm going to be making something homemade which is vanilla fudge."

Cecil says,

"Oh, I love vanilla fudge."

And I say, "That's why it's a good idea because *everyone* loves fudge. I am buying all the ingredients myself because otherwise it would feel more like a present from our pantry than from me.'

Mol says,

"That's very thoughtful of you, Clarice Bean."

I say, "Plus we don't have condensed milk or vanilla extract or the right kind of butter and also there isn't much sugar in the jar and these are the essentially vital ingredients."

Cecil says, "I see the problem."

Betty says, "What will you put the fudge in?"
And I say, "That's the other problem.

Gift boxes, it turns out, are much more
expensive than the gift to go in them."

Mol says, "This is so often true."
Then she thinks a bit and suddenly says,
"I might have the perfect idea for you."
And she does.

It involves cutting paper into slices and
weaving it back together and like
magic you have a TINY basket in the
shape of a heart, which is also
a tree decoration.

It looks tricky but it is simple and
Betty and me make a zillion of them,
or at least eighteen even though I don't need
that many. While we work we are chatting about
other things, mainly to do with fish.

After that, me and Betty go and sit in her
room on beanbags and we talk about the **RUBY
REDFORT LONG-DISTANCE WALKIE-TALKIES**
we both want, and I tell her all about my list. And
how I am wondering why Mom and Dad always

say that Christmas lists must be sent up the chimney on Christmas Eve because it doesn't leave much time for Santa to shop.

Betty says, "What are your parents talking about? You CAN'T send your list Christmas Eve. You have to send it much earlier than that."

And I say, "I know. It's one thing finding a piano at the last minute because I expect he keeps those in stock, but those **RUBY REDFORT WALKIE-TALKIES** are very popular and I worry they will have all sold out by then."

Betty says, "Also chimneys are very unreliable. You must use an actual mailbox and a first-class stamp. No one uses chimneys these days."

I say, "This is probably the whole reason why I NEVER get what I ask for."

She says, "Exactly. He needs more warning."

And I say, "I wonder why my mom and dad don't want him to have more warning?"

And Betty says, "It's very strange. It's almost as if maybe they DON'T want you to have a piano or a fish tank."

I say, "I know!"

Betty says I might as well take out the bit asking for snow because Santa ISN'T in charge of the weather, which makes me wonder who is.

Then I tell Betty my other worry, which I have to whisper in case Santa can hear. I say, "Sometimes I wonder, what if

you-know-who is NOT, in actual fact, real."

Betty looks confused so I whisper,

"Am I believing in NOTHING?"

Betty says, "What makes you wonder that?"

And I say, "Because I have never seen him."

Betty says, "But you're not SUPPOSED to see him."

I say, "But I have never even

heard an elf whispering."

And Betty says, "But elves are very quiet. They are trained to NOT make a sound." Then she says, "Just because you CAN'T see something or hear something DOESN'T mean it isn't there."

And this is true because think of a i r.

Betty says, "You don't have to stop believing in Santa. You just need a backup plan."

I never get to hear what the backup plan is because before Betty can tell me there is the sound of the doorbell pipes and there is my dad on the doorstep.

So I'm left in suspense as to what the backup plan might be. It's the kind of thing that happens to Ruby Redfort all the time but rarely happens much in real life.

★ ★ ★

When Dad and I get home, Minal is still going on about a fox in the yard, but every time we look there isn't one. Foxes is all my brother can talk about if he's not talking about macaroni.

Dad is looking in the fridge and he says,

"Where is that nice cheese I bought?"

Minal says, "The fox ate it."

Dad is quite mad about this.

He says, "Foxes DON'T even eat cheese."

Minal says, "This one does."

Dad says, "It's been a very tiring day, and I'm too exhausted to argue or discuss the problem of

cheese-eating foxes.
Let's just eat cookies
on the couch."

I am about to point
out the sign Mom
wrote asking us
NOT to eat
on the couch due
to cᵣumᵇˢ and mice,
but Dad DOESN'T
look like he's in the
mood for it.

NO EATING
on the COUCH
due to SPILLAGES
and crumbs.

★ ★ ★

When I say good night to Grandad, I hear his
radio say,

"Strong winds still predicted

which luckily reminds me to go and light the
Advent candle so I can wish against wind and for
snow. Of course I can only blow it out when it
has burned down to the right number,
which means I'm still up when Mom gets home,
so I am in hot water for NOT being in bed.
   I lie there thinking about the Moodys and all
the things we talked about and what call-me-Mol
said about good things falling apart so better
things can fall together.
   I gradually drift off with this thought in my
head, and I am sure I will dream of snow
                        and pianos
                              and socks with toes.

But actually I dream of foxes
sitting in the kitchen, eating
our Christmas dinner.

for Christmas, "

FOUR

Hark
How the Bells

DESPITE THE FOX IN MY DREAMS, I WAKE up actually in an exceptionordinarily happy mood. Because, you see, my Christmas hopes are much less squashed since I saw Betty and Cecil and Mol.

That's the thing about the Moodys—
    they always make you feel hopeful.

I'm not really a schoolish person normally, but I'm looking forward to today because it's the last day of it before vacation.

My main problem with school is Mrs. Wilberton. She is my teacher and I really wish she was Mrs. Nesbit.

The reason I do not get along with Mrs. Wilberton is because I tend to be in her bad books.

You see, I am NOT a good speller or a good dividerer, and unfortunately these are two things which Mrs. Wilberton thinks are more important than life itself. If you can't spell things the way the dictionaries want to spell things, or you can't divide 145 by 17, then Mrs. Wilberton will NOT be your biggest admirer.

Anyway, today is different because nothing needs to be spelled or divided—it just has to be decorated, and that's what I'm good at.

There are no classes, and you just have to watch a Christmas movie while you eat a cookie on the gym mats.

I wish school could always be like this. I am out of bed before my alarm clock has even told me to wake up. I remember what call-me-Mol said yesterday about focusing on the good things. And I wonder if I can make the good things more by also *doing* good things.

So while I am brushing my teeth, I clean the sink. It's easy to do with one hand—

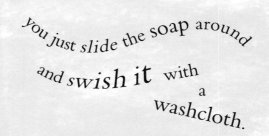

you just slide the soap around
and *swish it* with a
washcloth.

I use Kurt's because
he **never** does.

I come

downstairs

in my

usual

way,

which is with a sweater half over my head. On school days I tend to get dressed on the move so I'm not late. I'm mostly always late. When I have managed to poke my head through, I am surprised to see Betty Moody is on the doormat.

This is very unusual because she never comes over before school since I am not on the way.

I say, "Hey, Betty, how did you get there?"

She says, "It's a long story," because that's exactly what Ruby Redfort's friend Clancy Crew would say, but actually it is quite a short one involving Minal answering the door but not bothering to tell me Betty is here—instead he is eating Sugar Puffs in the kitchen.

Betty is too polite to just run upstairs to my room because it is still quite early in the morning and some of us are cutting it close and still in pajamas. Betty says she has come over with the backup plan,

which is basically lots of pieces of paper with
the same thing written on all of them.

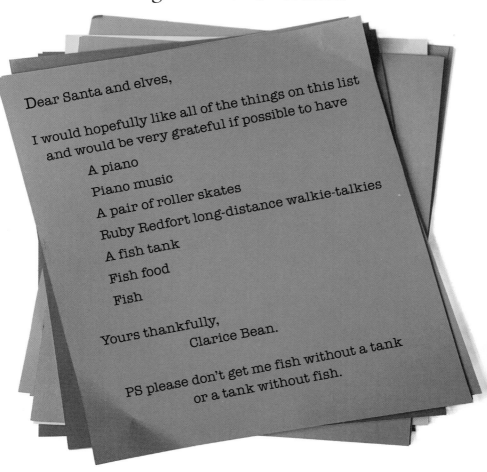

Dear Santa and elves,

I would hopefully like all of the things on this list
and would be very grateful if possible to have

    A piano
    Piano music
    A pair of roller skates
    Ruby Redfort long-distance walkie-talkies
    A fish tank
    Fish food
    Fish

Yours thankfully,
        Clarice Bean.

PS please don't get me fish without a tank
or a tank without fish.

Betty says, "Leave the list lying around so
that your mom and dad also see it and have a

chance to buy you the piano and everything, just in case Santa is NOT interested and/or NOT in existence."

I say, "What if I end up with two pianos?"

Betty says, "You can return one and get a credit."

I say, "What's a credit?"

Betty says, "It's like a check you can exchange for something that costs the same amount as the unwanted piano."

I say, "In that case I hope I get two pianos."

Betty says, "But remember you can only spend it in the musical-instrument shop, so you might have to end up choosing a harp or a trumpet, since they are unlikely to have much else."

This doesn't bother me because I have always been interested in owning a harp.

Betty and me find some good places to casually leave my lists so people can accidentally read them. We put one above the bathroom sink taped to the mirror. One is stuck to the TV and one on Mom and Dad's bedroom door and one inside Mom's purse. These seem the most likely places to

grab people's attention without meaning to.
We also stick one up the chimney just in case
Santa prefers to get his mail this way. You never
know.

There is no time for breakfast, so I take one of
Kurt's organically made energy bars and a piece
of cheese for flavor, which is exactly what
Ruby Redfort would do in my shoes.

★ ★ ★

This year at school we are having another carol
concert. Mrs. Wilberton always announces it
like it is a big surprise and a completely new
invention that she has come up with even though
people have probably been having carol concerts at
their schools for thousands or even millions of
years since the dawn of time.

The thing Mrs. Wilberton is trying to teach is
learning to sing in harmony. She says that,
in fact, I, Clarice Bean, do NOT have a
harmonic type of voice and I am
sending everyone else out of tune.

She says I need to "pipe down considerably."

I think this is unfair coming from someone who has a voice that is the sound of constant droning. At least my voice can go up and down— she only has one note and it is FLAT. Mrs. Wilberton is more excited than usual because our school is singing at the Julia Moggan Concert Hall, which is extremely old and also historical. Mrs. Wilberton is very proud of herself, but it is actually, in fact, thank you to Betty's dad, because he came up with the idea and organized it. He is a musician and plays in a very important orchestra, which is famous for music.

Lots of people will be there—not just the family ones but people who are actually expecting it to be good.

We have to wear gold or silver capes, and some of the parents and people have made these from fabric given by Arnie Singh's mother, who has kindly donated it.

Mom is bringing a group from the old people's center and Grandad and his friend Peggy will also be coming.

Peggy is Grandad's "Betty Moody," and she lives not too far from our house so they see each other most days.

Peggy used to be a singer, but she says her lungs aren't what they were, although they seem very good to me. She says she will give me some tips on tunefulness. She says it's all in the breathing. I was hoping I would be given one of the solo-ish parts of "The Twelve Days of Christmas" since I've gone to a lot of effort to learn what comes after the seven swans are swimming.

I would even do the eleven or so pipers piping part, but Mrs. Wilberton has decided to

get twelve other children solos, and I am only
allowed to join in with everyone else when my
voice will be drowned out by Robert Granger.
Robert Granger lives next door
and is annoying.

★ ★ ★

At recess I give out all the rest of my
Christmas cards to the people in my
class, including Grace Grapello and Cindy
Fisher, who are both quite surprised but also
pleased. And I can see how Mom is right that
being *generous* to the people you think don't like
you can have a good effect.

We all have to be outside on the playground
even though it is very cold and you can hardly
get your fingers to grip a jump rope—it is
important to jump when the
temperatures are freezing,
otherwise you could
seize up and perish.

If Ruby Redfort was at our school, she would start a campaign to prevent children from being forced outside in icy conditions. This is what's good about Ruby: she is an activist and won't take cruelty to children for an answer.

Winter is the only time I am just waiting for the school bell to ring and tell me: class has re-begun. You may THAW OUT. I have to defrost before I can even pick up a pencil.

Even though this is finally and actually the last day of school before Christmas, it is *not* the last day of seeing Mrs. Wilberton, since she will be popping up again at the Christmas concert, so it's not quite a real goodbye.

When we all flurry out of the school gates, Karl Wrenbury is

DRAGGING

his feet along

WITHOUT

cheerfulness.

It turns out he is down in the dumps because his younger brother, Alf, is home with a flu-ish cold and so cannot be outside. This means Karl cannot do his dog-walking job with his mom because someone has to stay home with Alf, and although Jean-next-door will be keeping an eye on things, Karl's mom says she needs Karl to keep an eye on Jean, who is often on the phone and NOT paying enough attention to Alf.

Karl's mom is a professional dog walker and walks several dogs all at once. Karl has two dog customers of his own, which is all he can manage until he is eleven and more experienced.

No one understands more about dogs than Mrs. Wrenbury, and she is teaching Karl everything she knows so he will very soon be an expert. He has been teaching my grandad about training Cement, and Grandad is at last making progress. He has actually stopped feeding Cement at the table, which Mom says she is very grateful to Karl for. Unfortunately, Cement does eat any old thing he finds on the floor, which is still a very bad habit. Karl says they will work on this behavior. Mom says she can't wait.

Karl says, "If I don't do my dog walking, then I won't save enough money to buy my Christmas presents and I will be letting everyone down, *including* my dog customers."

I know how he feels.

I say, "I don't know how I'm going to have enough money to buy all the ingredients for my vanilla fudge."

Karl says,

"I don't like fudge."

Then he just keeps on talking like this is a normal thing to say, even though I have never, ever met anyone who has ever said this before. Because who doesn't like fudge?

I am so in SHOCK about this that I can't concentrate on anything he is saying, so I mainly just walk along and nod, but his words aren't going into my ears. All I can think about now is this new problem on my plate.

What am I going to get Karl?

And *how* when I have no extra money left in the toadstool and I still need $7.99 plus a stamp

if I'm going to have enough to purchase the
RUBY FLY LIGHT?

Imagine NOT liking fudge.

At the end of our street, I have to walk past
Mrs. Stampney and she DOESN'T say, "By the
way, thank you, Clarice Bean, for the handmade
Christmas card. How kind of you to think of me
even though I am very mean and crabby." What
she DOES say is, "Could you tell that brother of
yours to turn his music down? It's very LOUD
and it's coming through the walls."

So I say, "Actually, it's my sister, Marcie,
who's the one playing the loud music."

Mrs. Stampney says, "Well, you can tell her from
me that the music she listens to is most unladylike!"

And I say, "I will definitely tell her. I know
Marcie will be very pleased to hear that.

Merry Christmas, Mrs. Stampney!"

And then I run along as quick as I can,
all the way home.

When I get in, Mom asks me how the last day
of school went.

I say, "Good."

She says, "So how did it go with your Christmas cards?"

I say, "Good."

She says, "Did it make Grace and Cindy happy that you made cards for them too?" and I say, "You know what, it actually really DID," and she says, "I told you so."

And I say, "It didn't work on Mrs. Stampney," and Mom says, "NOTHING does."

Mom is busy making some cupcakes. She says she has to bake at least seventy, which is a lot. They are for the party at the old people's center.

She says, "I have a horrible feeling I miscalculated the quantities and they may turn out to be soufflés or, even worse, cookies."

I say, "I think cookies are nicer than cupcakes," and she says, "Thank you."

I say, "Don't worry, I bet everyone will eat them anyway, whatever they taste like."

She says, "To be honest, I am past caring. I'm just looking forward to sitting down on a couch covered in crumbs with my feet up."

And this makes me feel bad because crumbs can

be quite uncomfortable, especially if you are wearing tights. So I start vacuuming.

And Mom calls out, "Clarice Bean,
I can't tell you what music it is to hear the drone of a vacuum cleaner."

And when she sits down, she says, "What a joy to sit in comfort. Thank you!"

And I say, "It's no big deal."

Which is what Ruby Redfort would say.

And Mom says, "Sometimes it's the SMALL things that make the BIGGEST difference."

Which is true because it turns out to have the benefit of seven dollars and ninety-nine cents in change lost under the cushions. If I'm allowed to keep it as mine, then I have enough to send off for the special-offer **RUBY FLY LIGHT** and *still* have exactly approximately the right amount for the fudge ingredients.

Mom says, "As far as I'm concerned, if you vacuum the couch, it's finders keepers."

Because there is not a moment to lose, I quickly put on my shoes and head out to the post office. Luckily, I have already filled out the coupon with my name and address, so I just hand over the money and the post office prints a money order, stamps the postage on, and sends it off.

Now all I have to do is cross my fingers that the **FLY LIGHT** will arrive before Betty leaves.

After supper, me and Grandad watch a program about wolves and how ALL dogs started off as wolves, but who could believe a Chihuahua was once a wolf?

And thinking about this reminds me of Frank, who is a Chihuahua that Karl walks, and then we start talking about Karl.

I say, "He is very in the dumps."

Grandad says, "And why's that, then?"

And then we talk about Alf's cold and Karl needing to stay home to keep him company while Jean-next-door is always on the phone.

I say, "Alf doesn't like being by himself with Jean-next-door because she forgets to talk to him, but if Karl stays home too, then Karl can't do his dog walking and can't save up his Christmas money."

Grandad says, "What a pickle."

And I tell Grandad how I am in the same boat for different reasons and have no money for Karl's present because he doesn't like fudge.

Grandad says, "Who doesn't like fudge?"

I say, "I know!"

Grandad says, "One thing that's worth thinking about is that a Christmas present doesn't have to be an actual thing—it can be a kindness or a helpful hand."

And then he says, "Sometimes it's the SMALLEST

things that make the BIGGEST difference."
And this is interesting because it's exactly
what Mom said.

Just before bed when I am brushing my teeth
Marcie comes into the bathroom. I step slightly
away from the sink so she can catch sight of
my Christmas list. I expect her to show some
interest, but all she says is "You'll be lucky."

She doesn't mean "I'm sure your wish will come
true." She actually means "For your information,
there is no chance of you getting any of this."

If I hadn't read **RUBY REDFORT**, then I might
agree with her point of view, but I have, so I know
she is wrong.

So I say the same thing Ruby Redfort would say:

"How can your wishes come TRUE,
if you NEVER even
bother to wish?"

FIVE

Joy to the World

IN THE MORNING I AM WOKEN LOUDLY by Marcie calling up the stairs. She has a very piercing voice and it comes right into my dream. She says, "**Peggy's on the phone for YOU.**" And I am very surprised because Peggy has never called for me before.

I *rush down* with bleary eyes.

Peggy says, "Clarice Bean, I've had a thought about your singing. Do you have a spare minute?"

And I say, "Yes."

And she says, "Then pop your warmest coat on and come right over," and I run to Peggy's as quickly as I can. There is a shopping cart parked in front of her gate and I have to twizzle it away before I can ring the doorbell.

When Peggy answers I say,

"Peggy, did you know there is a

shopping cart lurking by your house?"

And she says, "Oh, not AGAIN!

There's someone who keeps leaving carts

in the street and it is driving me

COMPLETELY around the bend."

We talk about this for a few minutes or so

and then Peggy says,

"Let's not waste our time with

abandoned shopping carts when there are

better things to think about.

How FAR can you count

on ONE BREATH?"

And I say,

"1 2 3 4 5 6 7 8 9 10 11 12 13 14 15 16 17 18 19 20 21 22,"

and she says,

"Not bad, but now let's do that again

without letting the numbers

run away from you."

We keep doing this over and over. I take a deep breath IN and I slowly breathe OUT the numbers until I have not the TINIEST bit of air left in me.

Peggy says, "If you keep practicing this exercise, you will find you can manage more numbers and they will sound less wobbly because you will be more IN CONTROL of your breath, which means the notes you sing will be STEADIER and more tuneful."

Then she says, "Take another breath and hold it— are you holding it?"

I just nod because I am, which means I can't speak.

"Imagine you are a balloon and the air is very s l o w l y hissing out through a GAP in your teeth. Make it last as L O N G as you can."

"H i S s S s S s S s s s S s S s s . . ."

I find I am very good at this. I think it's because I was a snake in the school play once. Hiss was the ONLY line I had.

Next, Peggy teaches me how to breathe right down into my actual toes.

You can tell if you're doing this right if you lie

on the carpet with your hands on your tummy. What should happen is when you breathe IN, your tummy fills up with air so it is sticking OUT, and then your chest fills up with air and you won't believe how much air you can get into your body if you use your stomach too. When you breathe OUT, you go completely FLAT.

After learning the breathing, Peggy teaches me how to warm up for singing, which is deep breaths with a yawn at the end because yawning opens up your throat.

I say, "It's a very strange thing to do, Peggy."

And she says, "You might NOT believe it, Clarice, but I have a singing friend, named Tiu de Haan, who warms up her voice by mooing."

I say, "Like a COW?"

She says, "Exactly. Tiu says she has mooed in all the most famous concert halls in the world."

I say, "Which should I do, mooing or yawning?"

Peggy says, "Moo when you are practicing making a BIG sound; yawn when you want to practice taking a BIG breath. Just don't worry what anybody else thinks—that's the trick."

"Now," she says,

"STAND
like
a
superhero,
very STRONG
and STRAIGHT,

imagining your cape *flowing* out behind you. Are you ready?"

"Ready," I say.

"So NOW we will sing!"

And we do.

When we have finished all our exercises, Peggy says, "You know, your Mrs. Wilberton is quite WRONG about your voice. You sing like an angel, Clarice Bean, and I will be sure to tell her so when I see her."

So of course I skip home in an utterly good mood.

Peggy is one of those people who always makes you feel good.

Grandad says this is a RARE talent.

I can see why Peggy is his best friend.

The phone is ringing and ringing when I get in. No one is answering it and I *rush* to pick it up before it gets bored and STOPS.

I say, "This is Clarice Bean speaking," and the phone says, "This is Granny speaking," back.

Me: "Oh, hello, Granny."

Granny: "Did you get a package?"

Me: "Yes."

Granny: "From New York?"

Me: "No."

Granny: "Bother!"

Me: "Why?"

Granny: "It should have reached you by now."

Me: "Oh."

Granny: "I think it's going to arrive very late."

Me: "How do you know?"

Granny: "My friend Wallace says there's some problem at the shipping company and that if they haven't managed to send your package by now, then it won't arrive until after Christmas."

Me: "Oh."

Granny: "I know."

Me: "Don't worry, Granny. It will be something to look forward to."

Granny: "Well, that's very kind of you to say, Clarice, because I am feeling dreadful about letting you all down like this."

Me: "It's not your fault."

I am feeling dreadful too because I can see our package for Granny NOT mailed. It's sitting there underneath Mr. Felixstow's Christmas charity package on the stool next to the fridge. Inside the box are all our Christmas presents for her in New York, including the TINY-USEFUL-THINGS BAG, and if no one mails it that will mean she has nothing to open from us. And we don't even have the true excuse of the shipping problem.

Our excuse is we can't be bothered to walk to the post office.

Granny and I talk about what's going on in her apartment building. Which is mainly that there is a loose rodent somewhere in the walls, but no one is sure what it is up to and whether it is alone.

Granny says, "How they get IN is what beats me."

I say, "Luckily we DON'T have this problem of wall rodents."

Granny says, "They can probably

smell Cement and this scares them off."

I say, "It would certainly scare me off if I was a rat with choices."

Cement has gotten into the habit of rolling in unpleasant things my dad says might have to do with foxes, so he is not smelling very pleasing, and Granny says, "I imagine not."

Once we have covered all the important things like:

> What I'm reading: **RUBY REDFORT**
> **CATCH YOUR DEATH**
>
> What she's reading: **How to Rid Your Home**
> **of Unwanted Pests and Rodents**
>
> What I am going to be WATCHING later
> What she's going to be WATCHING later
> What we are having for DINNER
> What she's having for LUNCH

we say goodbye, which takes a few tries because we always remember one last thing we forgot to remember, and of course I say, "We will call you on Christmas Day."

And she says, "I will be waiting by the telephone."

It is only when I put the phone down that I realize I have accidentally been nibbling the edges of the lemon drizzle cake. It might not matter except there is a note next to it that says:

Clarice Bean
Please do NOT nibble the edges of the LEMON DRIZZLE cake.

I hope no one notices.

Then I dump out the emergency money from the just-in-case can, find the pre-addressed labels, grab Granny's Christmas package and Mr. Felixstow's Christmas package, put them in Grandad's shopping cart, and *run like the wind* to the post office. Luckily the wind is going my way.

I stick the labels on the packages. Mr. Felixstow's package isn't too bad, but Granny's weighs a ton, and I only have just enough money to cover the stamps and have

a bit left over for

a

Yogga-Pop.

On my way out of the post office, I bump into Marguerite—who is my aunt but we just call her Marguerite. She is pushing her bike with the cart thing on the front that my cousin Yolla sometimes sits in. Today it is not filled with Yolla but with lots of stacked-up food in dishes and pots.

Marguerite looks utterly weighed down with shopping bags and has given up cycling. She's just trudging along.

She says, "I can't cycle against this wind."

I say, "Where are you going?" and she tells me she is delivering to the old people's center because it is their Christmas party today and, since she has a day off from work, she is helping out.

I say, "I can put some of the things in my cart if you like."

And she says, "I can't say I couldn't use the help."

So that's what we do, and she looks relieved.

She says, "It's such a shame we WON'T be seeing you on Christmas. We are going to miss you all so much."

I say, "Why don't you come?"

She says, "Well, if only
we hadn't made our
Christmas plans
back in January,
we would have
invited you ALL
to our place."

I say, "Do you always make your Christmas plans in January?"

And she says, "Not normally, but our friends the Robertses asked us five days after Christmas, when we were feeling like we'd really had enough of it all and the idea of being somewhere else with other people doing all the cooking sounded lovely."

Marguerite doesn't look like someone who is thinking this is a lovely idea.

She says, "The thing is, Clarice Bean, and I know I shouldn't say this . . ."

Marguerite always says "I know I shouldn't say this" when she is about to tell you something you are not normally told by a grown-up.

So I wait and she says, ". . . but I sort of wish we weren't going."

I say, "What about Al?"

Al is my uncle but we always just call him Al.

And she says, "He wishes we weren't going."

I say, "Me too."

She says, "I wish we were coming to *you*."

I say, "Me too."

She says, "The Robertses are fun, but . . ."

I say, "I know." Although I don't know because

I have never even heard of the Robertses.

And she says, ". . . and actually I love doing all the cooking," and I say, "I know."

"And it's so far to drive . . . and we will have to leave on Christmas Eve . . . early . . . very early."

I say, "Oh," because I don't know what to say. But it doesn't matter because I think she is talking to herself more than me.

She says, "I love Christmas Eve but we'll be in the car for most of it . . . and Noah gets so carsick . . . we will be stopping and starting."

I am listening to her and you can see she feels like she is already in the car and it does not look like a nice place to be.

I say, "Maybe something good will happen and the Robertseses will get terrible stomach bugs and ask you not to come because they don't feel like cooking!"

Marguerite seems very cheered up by this thought. She is smiling a LOT—she almost looks like she might laugh.

Then she says, "Speaking of cooking, you

should see what I have made for the center—I
hope they will like it."

I say, "Well, I know they will be really pleased,
because you are an exceptionOrdinarily
good cook."

And she says, "Well, thank you, Clarice
Bean. You have cheered me up completely."

When we arrive at the center,
Mom says, "Fancy seeing you
here, Clarice Bean."

And Marguerite says,
"She has been
such a help."

Once I have unloaded the
cart and all the other
things, I decide to stay
at the center and help
Marguerite set up the
table and heat the
dishes and serve all
the food with
her and Mom
and Reg.

Marguerite says, "It's lucky I ran into you,
   Clarice Bean. You have made my day."
And I feel the same because all my good deeds
are bringing back the Christmas spirit.

Mom says she is very glad to have an extra pair of
hands because it is hard to serve lunch and talk
to all the residents and make sure everyone is
having a good time.

I like the
      chatting.

I chat with Mr. Flanders, mainly about cookies,
      but then we both wonder if there is
   going to be life on Mars.

I also chat with Brenda, who has
      a tricky ingrowing toenail.

I know lots of the residents and they tend to
tell me interesting things like this.

★ ★ ★

Once we've cleaned up, we walk home together.
I tell Mom about mailing the packages.

And she says, "Goodness, Clarice Bean,
you *have* been spreading the Christmas spirit
today!"

And when Dad gets back, she tells him about this
too, and about helping Marguerite, and serving
lunch at the center.

And it is a perfect Christmas moment like one
of those cards where the families are smiling
at each other in front of the fireplace, except
Minal points at me and says,
"Clarice has been nibbling the edges off the
lemon drizzle cake when you aren't looking."

So I have to pinch him on the leg of course,
which takes me down a notch,

though it's NOT MY FAULT.

Mom looks inside the emergency can for cash
so she can send Kurt to the store for fish fingers.
She says,

"Where's all the just-in-case money?"

I say I spent it on the postage for the packages to Granny and Mr. Felix-whatsit.

And she says, "Wasn't there any change left over?"

I say, "No, it came to quite a lot in the end, and there was only enough left over for one Yogga-Pop."

And she says, "Goodness, that was expensive— I know the package to Mr. Felixstow was very heavy, but even so . . ."

I say, "It was Granny's package that was the expensive one."

And Mom says, "But that one was so light. Postage must have gotten a lot more pricey lately."

I am beginning to get a slight worry that something might have gone wrong with the labeling. So I decide the best idea is not to think about it.

Kurt goes off to buy the fish fingers and everyone is in a good mood and there are chips before dinner. Dinner is very nice and everyone is allowed as much ketchup as they want.

Afterward, we all squash onto the couch to watch the second part of the **RUBY REDFORT CHRISTMAS SPECIAL,** but the suspense is interrupted by Cement, who is barking at the not-blown-out Advent candle, which is still flickering on the table.

Grandad says, "I think he gets very stressed by flames."

Mom says, "Yes, I think it's ever since the wok caught fire."

I jump up and *run* into the kitchen to *blow* it out, but Minal gets there first. And then we get into an argument. Which ends up with us grabbing sleeves and *slipping* on the floor.

By the time I have given Minal an arm twist and he has given me a bruise on the leg, I have completely MISSED nearly the whole last four minutes of the **RUBY REDFORT CHRISTMAS SPECIAL**. I race back just in time to hear Ruby say,

"Tell it to the elves,
SUCKER!"

I have no idea who the "SUCKER" is,
but I think it
might
be
me.

SIX

Merrily on High

AT BREAKFAST IT IS JUST ME AND GRANDAD listening to the Christmas songs on the radio, eating our Sugar Puffs. I'm not sure where everyone else has gone, but it is very quiet except for the tree branch outside, which keeps tapping at the window. Grandad says he's had an idea.

He says,

"I asked Peggy about it and she said
she thought it was a good one."

And I wait for him to tell me what the idea is.

Grandad says, "I ALWAYS trust Peggy.
She always knows what's right,"

and then he starts talking about something else Peggy once said when he lost his keys in the park.

It is a very long story, which is rambling on
and making me fidget.

So I say, "Grandad, WHAT is your idea that
Peggy agrees is a good one?"
He says,
"Help walk the dogs."
I am not sure what he is talking about, but then
Mom comes out of the pantry and says,
"He means Karl's dogs
and Karl's mother's dogs—
if *you* help walk them,
then Karl can earn his Christmas money
and Mrs. Wrenbury can stay home
with Karl's brother and this can be
your Christmas present to Karl."
I say, "But two of us isn't enough,"
and Grandad says,
"But me and Peggy will help,
and together we would be able to manage
his two dog customers as well as
his mother's five dog customers
and Cement.'
It is a very remarkable idea and I agree with it.

So Grandad calls Karl's mom and she says,
"Yes, that will really cheer him up."
Then she says, "And you know what?
I would love to stay home with Alf
and watch the Muppets."

And so me and Grandad and Cement walk over
the hill to the block where Karl lives. We can
see Karl and his mom waving to us from the
second-floor balcony. Alf is waving next to them
in a pom-pom hat and a far-too-big coat.
Karl's mom calls down,
"Karl knows where to pick up
the dogs, so he will lead the way."
Grandad calls back, "Righto."
Karl's mom calls out,
"I can't tell you what this means to Karl."
Karl makes a stupid face at his mom, and Karl's
mom pulls his hat down over his eyes.
And she calls out,
"Thanks so much!"
and Alf calls out, "Thanks so much."

Then she shouts,
  "Now we are going to watch the Muppets,"

    and Alf shouts,
      "Now we are going to
        watch the Muppets,"

and they turn to go back indoors

    and Alf shouts,
"And we're going to make some paper chains,"

    and Karl's mom shouts,
      "And make paper chains."

We collect all the various seven dogs from their houses and then

we go to meet Peggy.

She is
sitting on
a bench
by
the park gate.

She says, "I'm wearing my best sweater."

I say, "So am I."

Peggy says, "That's good.

A singer must take care of their lungs—
keep the chest warm."

It's not actually that cold, but it is very *blowy* on the hill and it is hard to walk seven dogs plus Cement all at the same time.

The SMALLEST one, which is a Chihuahua named Frank, is finding it very difficult to walk because he is being *blown* to a STOP and is mostly stationary, so in the end Peggy puts him in her shopping bag

and Frank looks relieved.

Karl says this is not a good thing to do on a regular basis but in an emergency it is OK.

It is a very nice day even with the wind, and there are lots of people and lots of dogs out today. Several of the dogs we meet on the hill are wearing Christmas coats and collars. One is a pug in antlers.

Karl does not really approve of antlers on a dog. He says, "Dogs are not toys."

I agree but secretly think if I had a pug I would put antlers on it.

Betty always dresses up her dog, Ralph, who is a Pekingese, and Ralph doesn't mind a bit—this year he will be a choirboy.

We won't tell Karl.

Peggy has brought her Thermos so we can all have a hot drink on a bench.

She asks Karl if he has done his Christmas shopping yet, and he says he's hoping to do it after the dog walking.

He wants to look in the stores to see if he can find some presents for his mom and his brother, Alf. He says, "I also want to get one for Mrs. Tomassini—she makes dinner for me and Alf on Tuesdays and Wednesdays when my mom has to work. She makes really nice things and she's teaching me to cook too."

Peggy says, "It's a wonderful thing to know how to cook."

He says, "I can do macaroni and cheese now. It's not a normal one—it's got all sorts of things in it."

I say, "It sounds quite advanced."

And he says,

"It's not as tricky as it sounds—
I'm sure you'd be able to do it.
You just have to know how."

And Peggy says,

"So what are you thinking of getting
Mrs. Tomassini for Christmas?"

Karl says,

"Well, I was thinking about
a wooden spoon, you know,
for stirring? But do you think
she might already have one?"

Peggy says,

"You can never have
too many wooden spoons
if you like cooking."

She says,

"Sometimes you can find
ones you can
hang up by a string."

Karl likes this idea.

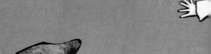

There is something about
the wind when it is warm
like this that makes you feel
like you want to RUN.
And we do, we ALL run

around and around and around.

The dogs look VERY happy too.
Karl says,
"It's easy to tell when a dog is happy—
it's all in their tails."
But I think you can also know from their faces.
To me it is obvious they are smiling,
and Peggy agrees.

After our walk, we drop off the dogs, and Grandad
gives Karl an envelope with *Merry Christmas*
written on it and says, "Just a little something
to say thank you for helping me
train Cement."

Grandad and Peggy go to the Polish café next to Eggplant for another cup of tea. Me and Karl wander along Park Road and he pops into stores while I stand outside with Cement, and then I pop into the corner store to buy my ingredients while Karl and Cement wait outside.

The last store is the kitchen store, and Karl is in there forever trying to choose a spoon.

I say, "What took you so long?" and Karl shows me the spoon and says,

"I wanted one that you can hang up by a string, but they didn't have any."

I say, "It's still very nice."

Karl says, "Do you think she will like it?" and I say, "I would," which is actually true even though I don't need a wooden spoon.

I invite Karl back for dinner, and Karl shows Mom the spoon and he says, "Maybe it's too boring."

And she says, "Not at all, but if you wanted to, we could drill a SMALL hole in the end of the handle.

I've got some striped
string you could
thread through it, and
then Mrs. Tomassini
could hang it up."
And Karl says, "That's exactly
what I was wanting!"
They work on it together
and he goes home really happy.
He shouts, "Thank you for the spoon help,
Mrs. Tuesday, and thank you for the
dog walking, Clarice Bean! It was a really
good Christmas present!'
It is so windy outside that his voice is almost
blown away, but I'm sure I can just hear
him say, "I've got a really good idea for your
Christmas present, Clarice . . .

Just wait and see!"

SEVEN

Christmas Tree, O Christmas Tree

TODAY IS MY SECOND-MOST-FAVORITE day before Christmas because it's the day we get our tree. We tend to get our tree a long time after everyone else on our street because Mom says if you get them too early they drop needles all over the carpet. Mom usually comes with us because she knows how big a tree is allowed to be before it won't fit in the room, but she can't come today because she is working at the old people's center again due to short staffing.

As she is leaving the house, she calls out,

"Remember, not TOO big!"

Dad and me and Minal go down to the Christmas tree place, which is basically a HUGE lot with nothing but trees everywhere.

Grandad is banned from coming on these trips because he always picks the sad trees. They are called the sad trees because Mom says they look like they are crying pine needles, i.e., they are already a bit dried up and on their last legs.

Most of the trees are all leaning on each other, tied up with string, which makes it hard to know what they will be like once they are freed.

So we look at the ones that are on display. There are so many to choose from I can't make up my mind.

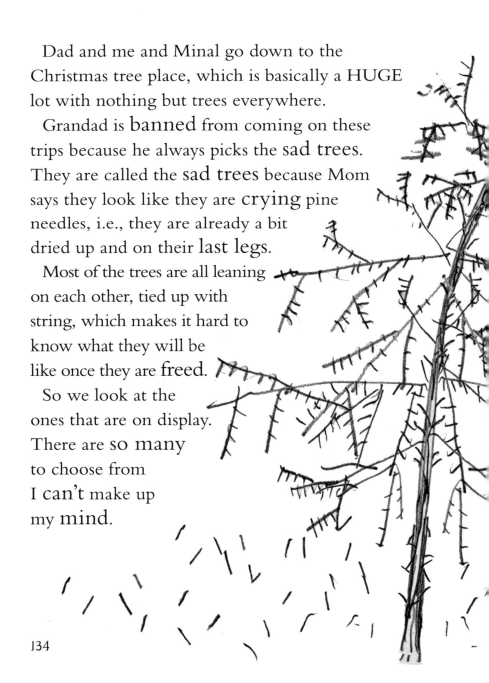

I wander around the trees,
        up and down the rows of them,
and I try NOT to touch any of them because
I don't want to give them hope that they are
the chosen one.

It is really hard to make the right choice because
they are different shapes from each other, and
some have nice gaps between the branches,
        and some have nice needles.

There are so many different breeds.
Although Dad says when you are talking about
trees you are supposed to say species.

He says, "Breeds is for dogs."

So I say, "Dad, how would you choose
        a species of tree?"

And he says, "Just pick one you think will
fit in the car."

This of course is NOT a good way to pick a
perfect tree, but luckily Dad bumps into
someone he knows from work named Mr. Oberon,
so I know we are going to be here forever,
        which means there is plenty of time
                to find the right one.

Since I would prefer to look in peace,
I decide it might be BEST
if I lose Minal.

I do this by hiding
for a minute in a clump
of perched-together
Christmas trees, and I can hear Minal Cricket

as he runs up and down, going,

"Where are you?
I'm going to
TELL Mom
if you don't
come out."

It's important to keep your breathing to a minimum and NOT sneeze if you want to keep out of your enemy's clutches. It's also a good idea to avoid chewing bubblegum. Ruby Redfort could tell you a lot about this, since she got captured once by several arch villains in the book **CATCH YOUR DEATH** and it was due to the smell of Hubble Yum bubblegum.

Thinking about Ruby Redfort makes me want to read my book, which, luckily, I have with me. I get so caught up in the plot, which is actually set in a forest, that I completely forget to look for trees.

★ ★ ★

When Dad finally finishes chatting, I reappear like magic, and he says, "So which tree is it going to be?"

And Minal says, "This one," and points to a tree that is twelve feet high.

Dad says, "That is not going to fit in our living room, let alone the car."

Minal starts whining. "But it's the best one!"

Dad says, "Jeepers, Minal, we can't even carry it."

So of course my brother tries to pick it up, which is not possible for someone who is a squirt.

It falls on top of him

and he is trapped underneath it.

Minal is making this weird sound and at first we think he is injured and in requirement of a medical assistant but then we realize it is the sound of trapped giggling.

Minal Cricket has a strange giggle which sounds more like a piglet than a boy. It is one of those catching types of laughs and Dad finds it very easy to contract laughing, so he is set off by Minal.

This makes the tree-selling man quite upset because all he can see from where he is, is a man who is more than forty laughing at a fallen-over Christmas tree.

I shout, "Don't worry! He is NOT laughing at the tree—he's laughing because there is a SMALL boy trapped under it."

This does not sound at all funny to the man and he starts getting agitated about safety and so Dad has to extract Minal on the double before we get reported to the child protectors.

Dad says, "Look, he's fine!"

When the tree-selling man sees that Minal is not injured, he gets even more upset, and Dad goes a bit pale-ish when he is informed that due to damage to several branches, we are going to have to buy this tree whether we like it or not.

The laughing is ended.

Dad goes quiet and says he is going in search of a cup of coffee because the idea of getting a twelve-foot tree into a less-than-twelve-foot car is sending his energy levels in a d o w n w a r d direction.

In the end we have to call Uncle Ted and ask him for his assistance. Uncle Ted is a firefighter so of course he is used to dealing with emergencies and getting a tree into a car should not be a problem. He has brought a saw with him and he chops

off some of the trunk and we sort of manage to
WEDGE it so it's mostly in the car but not quite
all. Uncle Ted ties Minal's sweater to the sticking-
out-of-the-car part as a warning that we are
dangerous. Minal is NOT pleased and starts
gribbling, but Dad explains that it is all his
own fault, so i.e. put a sock in it.

On the drive back I find myself sitting in the
branches and I have an idea of what it might
be like to be a squirrel.

When we get home there is a realization that the
tree is very big and more than was expected in as
far as how much it sticks out.

We have to move most of the furniture to the
sides. When Mom gets home from work she has to
walk *sideways* into the room.

Everyone is waiting for her to say something with
her arms folded and a lemon-lip look, but when
she sees Dad's face, which seems a bit down in
the eyes, she just says,

"I think it's nice to bring the outside in."

And everyone looks relieved and has a cup of tea.

But the problem is that we
now have a very large tree
in our house which is
not allowing us to
sit comfortably
in chairs,

and it's hard to
see around the
branches.

Minal and me have started another argument about the tree, which is not my fault.
I only pointed out that he is to blame and should be in trouble. Marcie has joined in by telling us we are both annoying so we tell her that this is none of her beeswax and Kurt tells us to shut up because we are ALL boring.

So now everyone starts SHOUTING.

Mom says,
    "Do you think we should put it outside? It could look nice in the yard."
    Uncle Ted says, "It might be a good idea because this tree is going to make it impossible for you to ALL be in the same room together."
    Dad says,
    "In that case let's keep it where it is."
    But then Grandad wakes up in his armchair and panics because he thinks he is lost in a forest. It takes him a few minutes to feel sure that he is indoors.
    Even so, he decides to put his coat on.

He says, "I'll have my tea out of the Thermos."

Mom says, "Why?"

and he says, "Because I always do when I'm outside."

Mom says, "You are in the living room."

He says, "I know you *say* that, but it doesn't feel like it."

Mom goes to get the clippers and does some pruning, which means we can move the furniture back to mostly where it's supposed to be.

Then she winds the lights from the top of the tree toward the bottom, only they run out in the middle and she says, "I'm going to need at least two more strings of them."

Uncle Ted offers to go and buy some more, but it is decided that he cannot be trusted to choose the right kind of tree lights, so Marcie is sent out grumbling.

Once that's decided, Mom has to start making supper, so I put all the decorations and thingummyjigs on the branches. The technique is to make sure that everything ISN'T all clumped together.

My favorites are the glass ones in different shapes, which are treasured heirlooms of the family. Some are elves and some are angels, and most of them are very old and from before I was born. I also like the felt ones, which are horses, and the wooden ones, which are toadstools. I don't know why toadstools are for Christmas, but they look good.

Mom says, "You have to spread them all evenly and don't just put all the nice ones on one side and the not-so-nice ones in the back."

I say, "Why do we bother having
            the not-so-nice decorations?"
and Mom says, "Because we are sentimental about them."

I'm not sure why she is sentimental about Minal's decorations—they are just macaroni and there is plenty of that in the pantry.

I get decorating and I am doing well with the spreading them out until something interesting comes on the television, and it is only when it's finished that I realize most of the decorations are facing the TV.

I am standing on a stool, trying to move some angels and elves to the other side of the tree, when I am almost

toppled off
by Minal, who starts jumping
up and down,
squeaking.

And I have to
GRAB on to the tree
to hold my balance,
and
I let go of several

elves and they

S M A S H

on the floor
and Mom rushes to rescue the tree from
falling completely over on top of me
and she bumps into Grandad's Thermos of tea,
which luckily is cold because it spills all over
Grandad's pant legs, and Mom loses her temper.

She says,

"Minal, *SHRIEKING*
and jumping UP and DOWN
is ABSOLUTELY banned!
Just LOOK what
you've done!"

And he says, "But I saw the fox,
like the one in my book."
And Mom says, "Your fox book is banned!"
And Minal says, "But—"
And Mom puts her finger up, which means
"No buts!"

and Minal is in the doghouse because he has
destroyed the ancient Christmas decorations.

There are no elves left, and they all have to be
sucked up into the vacuum cleaner, and Grandad's
pants have to come off.

Mom looks sad about the elves. She says,
"They belonged to my grandmother,"
and I say, "And now they are gone forever."

And Mom sighs in a deep way and says, "Oh
well, they gave us great joy while they lasted."

But I didn't want them to stop lasting
and I wish they could be put back together
because I'm not sure we can do without elves.
Because, you see,

everyone

needs

elves

at
Christmas.

EIGHT

Deck the Halls with Boughs of Holly

IT IS THE DAY BEFORE CHRISTMAS EVE and it is the day of the school carol concert.

All the shopping has been done—except for Dad's. He hasn't started his yet, but that's normal and Mom doesn't even pretend to be surprised.

Mom and Dad have to go out somewhere and they have asked me to be in charge of answering the door to the turkey person because Kurt will have his headphones on and Mom says, "There is not a chance he will hear the doorbell ping." She says, "When it arrives, shout up to your brother and get him to take it out back to the fridge in the shed."

She says, "You will need help because your father accidentally ordered the massively LARGE one."

Dad says, "Whatever you do, do not try to squeeze the turkey into the fridge in the kitchen or it will be chaos."

They have also asked me to be in charge of making a cup of tea and a slice of lemon drizzle for Mrs. Rippon, who has "kindly offered to come at a moment's notice to do a one-off clean and polish of all the floors." Dad says the floors are so dirty that they are a danger to germs.

Mom says, "I've baked a fresh lemon drizzle cake so please *do not nibble it!*"

Mom says she feels she can trust me to do all this because it seems at last some of Betty Moody's responsible influence has rubbed off on me. She doesn't have much choice because Marcie and Grandad and Minal are going to be in and out for most of the day, coming and going, and Mom says she has lost track of who's home when, so it's all up to me.

She says, "Mrs. Rippon will let herself in with her key."

Then mostly everyone goes out and the house is quiet. I want to prove that I am to be trusted because it gets you extra points with Santa and you need a lot of points to get a piano, so I decide to wait on a stool by the door. That way I won't miss the turkey's arrival. I've got my **RUBY REDFORT** word-searcher puzzle book so it's not as boring as you might think.

By the time the doorbell rings, I am very desperate to use the bathroom. I have to *run* for it as soon as I've wished *a very merry Christmas* to the turkey person, who is a woman who turns out to be very chatty and has a holly pin that flickers.

I shout up to Kurt, but Mom and Dad are right and he does NOT hear a blimming thing and I can't be bothered to go and yell through his bedroom door because he will just grumble.

The turkey is very hard to move so I have to take it out of its box and carry it like a heavy baby wrapped in paper.

I think about taking it down to the shed in the wheelbarrow, but it is raining, so instead

I am pleased because there is no chaos at all and so now I can think about having a little sit-down before Mrs. Rippon takes over the kitchen.
Of course, that's when I realize that the lemon drizzle is now stuck BEHIND the turkey. Mom put it in the fridge to hide it from nibblers.

I have to cautiously open the door and feel around with my hand. The cake is WEDGED in the back and I can only get to it by maneuvering the turkey outward and dropping it on the floor.

I am wondering how I am going to get the energy to pick it up, when the doorbell rings. Since I am expecting no one else to answer it, I have to.

And there is the postman with a large elastic band full of letters. I am hopeful that the **RUBY FLY LIGHT** will be one of them, but it is NOT there.

ALL except one are addressed to the Tuesday family, which is us, so I am allowed by law to open them. It takes quite a while and by the time I have arranged the cards all over the place, I realize I have completely forgotten I was supposed to be lifting a turkey off the floor.

I run back to the
kitchen, but strangely
the turkey is NOT
where I left it and has
moved itself to the back
door. It doesn't look quite
the same shape as it did
before—something oddish
has happened and it has a
nibbled look. I think it has
definitely been chewed
by possibly a dog and is
NOT fit for human
consumption, especially
because the kitchen floor
is still a hygiene hazard.

I instantly

have

a **bad** feeling

and am

FROZEN

with panic.

Ruby Redfort says PANIC will freeze your brain, and of course she is right, and I sit at the table for a few minutes STARING at the lemon drizzle, wondering what to do.

Ruby often says that when you fear for your life, it is a good idea to go to your nearest safe space. So I shut myself in the downstairs bathroom. It is not actually my actual safe space but it has a lock and a toilet.

I am thinking Dad was right about not putting a too-big turkey in a full fridge and how it is now chaos.

While I am locked in, I hear quite a lot of different-size footsteps plus slippers passing by, which is the sound of Mrs. Rippon.

Minal is gabbling on at her about foxes, and so I decide to stay put until I can make a clean getaway.

I only manage to distract myself from possible doom by doing fifteen or so word searches. One of the words in the searches is CAKE, and this reminds me how I would love a slice of lemon drizzle. I want it so much I can almost taste it, which is when I realize that actually I *can* taste it because I must have accidentally nibbled the corners while panic was FREEZING my brain. I am already in enough trouble due to the chewed turkey without Mom finding out about the cake-nibbling.

So as soon as I hear Mrs. Rippon leave without a cup of tea, I unlock the door and tiptoe into the kitchen.

No one is there and so I slice the nibbled bit of cake and quickly eat it before anyone can know. This is called EATING THE EVIDENCE and is what Ruby Redfort would advise me to do in this situation.

Mom will think Mrs. Rippon has eaten it and will never know that it was me.

Then I duck upstairs into the linen closet. While I am waiting in there, I am thinking about my unfortunate situation and what I can do to wriggle out of it.

I am tempted to add a TURKEY to my Santa list, but this might arouse suspicion. Ruby Redfort says: If you are trying to avoid arousing suspicion, then you must act NORMAL.

Acting normal means **not** talking about turkeys and how much one might cost.

So I will do exactly as Ruby says:

RULE #1: KEEP IT ZIPPED

i.e., keep your trap shut.

When I finally come out and take a good look around, I notice that the floor is very shiny and there is no sign of a turkey.

Not anywhere.

I can't see it in the kitchen fridge or the shed fridge and I am utterly lost for ideas of where it could have gone to.

Granny often says "Dwelling on things you can't fix can make you very unhappy" and "Sometimes it's best to

put problems behind you,"

so this is what I do.

It is very good advice because no one says a word about the missing bird.

Mom asks if I made Mrs. Rippon a cup of tea and I do a sneeze and say *yes*.

She LOOKS at me with suspicious eyes but she DOESN'T say ANYTHING.

So **perhaps** everything's going to
turn out well

after all.

NINE

Sing Choirs of Angels

AT FIVE O'CLOCK IT IS TIME TO PUT ON coats and get going. I am traveling to the school carol concert with the Moodys.

Call-me-Cecil is taking us because he also has to be there early as a performer, and me and Betty have to be there early to do our warming-ups.

Everyone is actually very excited except for Robert Granger, who has forgotten his silver cape. Luckily, Mrs. Singh has brought a spare one along so the whole thing is NOT ruined.

When it gets to 5:55 we all have to be quiet and shuffle onto the stage. The audience is there and sitting on chairs without talking, and the Julia Moggan Hall is all in the dark with NO lights, just candles and . . .

an exceptionOrdinarily
BIG Christmas tree,
even bigger than ours.

Mrs. Wilberton won't trust children with real candles, so we have to use those plastic ones that pretend to flicker but are battery powered. I think plastic candles aren't really the spirit of Christmas, but the people in the audience don't seem to mind and are carried away by the singing.

I am standing next to Karl Wrenbury and Toby Hawkling, who I can tell you aren't singing the correct words, but luckily no one can hear or they would be sent outside with their coats on.

When it gets to "The Twelve Days of Christmas," Mrs. Wilberton looks pinched in the face. This is due to my cousin Noah, who is supposed to be the partridge in the pear tree but is instead *wilting* on a chair. He looks like he already has car sickness, and it is probably just the thought of the nine hours' drive to see the Robertseses on Christmas Eve which has made him want to vomit.

Thoughts definitely can have a BAD effect.

You can hear the fidgeting in the audience
because there is a gap between the singing that
is NOT meant to be there, and I can tell
Mrs. Wilberton is beginning to PANIC.
Mrs. Wilberton says,
"We need a NEW partridge
in a pear tree, *quick sticks!*"
I put my hand up.
She is squawking in a wobbly voice and says,
"Any volunteers who know the part!"
And I shout, "ME!"
But even though she is looking right at
me, she doesn't seem to see me and
I am utterly ignored.
In the end it is decided that I will
not be swapped in at the last minute
but Audrey Broadley will. At first she
is really good but halfway through she
does get muddled up with the various
numbers of birds and Mrs. Wilberton
goes very *HARSH* in the eyes
and if I were Audrey Broadley I would
NOT stay for the gingerbread men.

Right at the very end the **pretend pear** falls off
the tree and **rolls** across the stage, and this puts
Audrey into a T R A N C E and she **forgets**
to **sing** the last *partridge in a pear tree*
and the song **can't finish**
without that and everyone
is **waiting**

   and waiting

sσ] sing it

because someone has to.

And Peggy stands up and
starts clapping and
everyone stands up
and starts clapping
and Grace Grapello
says, "I didn't **know** you
had such a good voice,
Clarice Bean," and I say,
"Thank you, Grace.
That's very nice of you to
say," which it is.

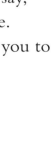

Afterward, when the lights are turned up and we've all gotten down off the stage,

Peggy says,

"Clarice Bean, you sing like an angel."

Dad says, "You didn't tell us you had a solo part," and Mom says, "Yes, that was a

wonderful surprise,"

and call-me-Cecil just winks.

Then there is a lot of chatting and Peggy says she's going off to find Mrs. Wilberton and Grandad says,

"I wouldn't want to be in *her* shoes."

People are allowed ONE gingerbread man per person and a hot drink out of a plastic cup. Due to environmental reasons and my mom and dad promising Kurt not to drink out of plastic cups they have to go thirsty. Dad has a choking episode with a gingerbread man that is rather dry, and he has to *rush off* to find a water fountain.

Marguerite, Al, and Noah say they have to *rush* back to the babysitter, who is at home with cousin Yolla.

Dad tries to persuade them to stop by for some
Christmas soup, but they say,
"We have such an early start in the morning
        that we must get straight to bed."
Mom says, "Make sure you call us when you
get to the Robertses," and they say, "We
certainly will!" and we all have to wish them
Merry Christmas in a hurry and this is sad because
we won't see them until it is all over. Even
sadder is that I can't give Betty her Christmas
present, and it was specially bought for the plane
trip.

Betty says, "It doesn't matter, Clarice Bean.
It will be something to look forward to."

Call-me-Mol says, "I know what we'll do—
as soon as we get back, you can all come over
for New Year's!"

This cheers us up like anything and we arrive
home in a very good mood and discover Mom
has put decorations up and down the stairs
and in the hall.

She says never forget the hall because that is
the most important place to have good cheer

and welcome people
to our home.

Unfortunately, Cement has had a terrible episode of the vomits all over the cleaned floor, and Dad says, "Well, that's a nice welcome home," and Mom says, "Whatever is the matter with that dog?" and Grandad says, "I think he swallowed some dirty puddle water in the park."

But even Dad cleaning something unpleasant off the floor cannot cause us to lose the good spirits we are all in.

Mom has made a very nice dinner, which is a purple soup and a baked potato.

She says, "Minal has kindly decorated the table."

For some reason Minal has chosen to make his decorations spiders, but I decide NOT to make a comment about this because I don't think this would be in the Christmas spirit even though spiders definitely DON'T have anything to do with Christmas.

Things are going very well and it is even agreed that we might play sevens after dinner. Sevens is a card game and everyone in my family likes playing cards and this includes us ALL.

But then the Christmas spirit is interrupted. Because Minal *knocks* his drink into Marcie's pudding and she is tipped over the edge.

This makes Kurt aggravated and he says she is overreacting as usual.

She says, "Well, at least I *can* react and don't just sit there like a potato."

He says something very RUDE to Marcie, which is NOT at-the-table language.

And Dad says, "That is not at-the-table language."

And I say, "Could I—"

And Dad says, "Do NOT repeat it, Clarice Bean!"

And Marcie says, "Yes, stay out of it."

I say, "I was only going to ask for the sugar," and Mom says, "I don't think this pudding needs more sugar; doesn't everyone agree?"

She is trying to change the subject.

But Marcie says, "Well, I wouldn't know because my pudding is under water."

Minal says, "It's just a *spilled* drink!"

She says, "OK, so you eat it, squirt!"

So he does and Marcie screeches.

I say, "Don't get your underwear in a bunch."

Which is what Ruby Redfort would say.

And Minal says, "You can't say underwear at the table."

And Kurt says, "What's wrong with underwear?"

And Marcie says, "If we are talking about yours, quite a lot, actually."

Mom says, "Children, children! Where is your Christmas spirit?"

Marcie says, "Minal drowned it."

Mom says, "Can everyone who doesn't like someone else NOT sit next to them?"

Dad says, "That's going to be difficult."

Mom says, "Can everyone who doesn't like someone else please leave the table?"

Grandad is left sitting
on his own.

Mom goes off to have some time to herself
in the bath.
Dad says he is going to stand in the backyard for
a while.
Everybody else goes to their own room
        and I climb into the linen closet.

Everything
is wrong.

The Christmas spirit has gone missing.
And when I go downstairs to get a glass of water,
        I find the Advent candle has
                burned down to the end.

It's definitely

NOT

going to

snow

now.

TEN

In the Bleak Midwinter

ON CHRISTMAS EVE I GET UP EARLY.
Getting up early is not normal for me, but
Christmas Eve is different from all the other days
and I never want to waste even a minute.

This year I can't *afford* to waste even a *second*
because I'm really behind with everything
due to being locked up in the bathroom when I
should have been finishing my Christmas-present
preparations, i.e., writing my gift tags. I run upstairs
to ask Mom if I may use the kitchen in privatude,
but I am not allowed to actually peep in the door
because she is wrapping presents in the TINY study
while talking to Granny on speakerphone.

I hear Granny say, "Yes, your Christmas package arrived. It's huge—I had to get the janitor to help me take it up to my apartment."

Mom says, "What do you mean huge?" She sounds like she has a funny look on her face, like she's trying to puzzle something out which cannot be puzzled. It is beginning to dawn on me that Mr. Felixstow might at this very moment be wondering what to do with a TINY-USEFUL-THINGS BAG and a macaroni necklace.

So I tiptoe in the other direction and look for Dad instead.

This takes at least twelve minutes because he is not in his usual place and is in fact in the yard, trying to stop a fence from *blowing away.*

When I tell him my plan, he asks if "using the kitchen will involve heat and/or sharp implements."

And of course it does because that is what a kitchen is mainly for.

He says I will need responsible supervision and he can't help because he's having trouble with the wind.

I explain how I *would* normally suggest Betty, since she is the most responsible person I know, but she is about to be off to Japan.

And Dad says,

"I agree. Betty Moody would have been a good choice as she is indeed one of the most responsible people any of us know, certainly more responsible than most of the people I work with, but in any case, it needs to be someone of at least sixteen or over."

So I choose Grandad because he is the one most likely to forget what we are doing and the only other person more than the age of a teenager.

Grandad says yes because of course he always does, even though he is busy doing a jigsaw puzzle on the coffee table. Lots of pieces have fallen on the floor, and I hope he finds them before Cement eats them.

I say, "Grandad, don't look at the name of what we are making, just the recipe."

He says, "Boiled sugar with vanilla, milk, and butter. Sounds delicious." Then he says, "I think we should wear aprons."

In the end we decide we should also wear swimming goggles just to be on the safe side, because, you see, sugar boils at 212 degrees Fahrenheit. I learned that from my science project.

Fudge sounds dangerous.

To begin with, you must put all your ingredients in a row and find the cooking scale, which is not in the cupboard where your mom said it would be and is actually in her bedroom where she has been weighing packages for the post office.

Making fudge is easy and also hard. It is not hard to do the recipe, which is mainly melting things together, but it *is* hard to make the fudge fudge-ish.

I don't think mine has turned into
what it is meant to turn into.
It is not crumbly and there is
nothing soft about it and
it has actually turned into
a disappointment.
Grandad says,
"I am certain
that—whatever
this is meant to
be—it is NOT a
disappointment."
It is nice of him
to say this, but
I don't think
it's true, since
I have to chop
it up with a
hammer, which
is NOT something
you normally
need to do
with fudge.

★ ★ ★

By lunchtime Dad is just preparing to go to the
stores and start his Christmas shopping.
He says having only four hours to get it done
concentrates the mind. Minal is making more
macaroni jewelry, and I go off to my room
to write my gift tags. On my way past the front
door, I find a puffy envelope addressed to me.
I open it and there is Betty Moody's Christmas
present, the one I sent off for, but sadly it is too
late because she is by now on her way to the
airport. I take it up to my room and open it and I
realize that it is even better than I thought it was
and most definitely worth the special offer of $7.99
and it is just what Betty would need on an eleven-
and-a-half-hour flight to Tokyo.

I am wondering which gift tag Betty would
like most—probably an elf on a toadstool—
when I hear Mom calling up the stairs in a
stretched voice,

"Does anyone know what has happened to
the turkey? It is NOT in the shed fridge."

And of course I am FROZEN with panic so I go quiet and pretend I haven't heard her.

And Mom shouts, "Marcie? MARCIE! MARCIE! Have YOU seen the turkey?"

Marcie: "What turkey?"

Mom: "What do you mean '*what* turkey'? The Christmas turkey. Do you know where it has gone?"

Marcie: "No."

Mom: "Kurt?"

Kurt: "Why would I know what has happened to the turkey? I'm a vegetarian."

Pause.

Mom: "Minal, have you seen the turkey?"

Minal: "Yes."

Mom: "Where is it?"

Minal: "I don't know."

Mom: "When did you *last* see it?"

Minal: "When it was on the floor."

Mom: "What?"

Minal: "On the floor."

Mom: "What was it doing on the floor?"

Minal: "It was being eaten by Cement."

Mom: "Cement ate the whole turkey?"

Minal: "No, the fox ate half."

Mom: "What fox?"

Minal: "The one who comes into the kitchen."

Mom: "Minal, can we please return to planet Earth for two minutes?"

Minal: "But . . ."

Mom: "When did you see a turkey on the floor?"

Minal: "Yesterday when Clarice was locked in the bathroom and, by the way, she nibbled the lemon drizzle cake."

Silence.

And then . . .

"Clarice Bean!"

But I have already climbed inside the
linen closet and am closing the door

and hardly
   taking
      a
    b r e a t h.

ELEVEN

It's Beginning to Look a Lot Like Christmas

I AM JUST WORRYING IF I WILL EVER BE able to come out, when Kurt peeks in and says, "The coast is clear."

I say, "How did you know I was in *here*?" and he says, "This is where you always go when you are in trouble."

Marcie says, "Don't worry, Clarice. They'll get over it."

Kurt says, "They'll forget about it."

I say, "They won't forget they had a turkey eaten by a dog."

Minal says, "You do know Santa isn't going to leave you any presents."

Marcie says, "MINAL!"

And Minal says, "But it's TRUE,

if you're bad he doesn't come."

Kurt says, "That's not true."

But I know that it's NOT not true—it is
a well-known FACT.

Marcie says, "I'll call Granny. She always has
good ideas for getting out of tricky situations."
And so Marcie calls Granny and explains about the
turkey trouble.

And Granny says, "Where is your mother now?"
and Marcie tells her how Mom has had to rush out
of the house without a second thought because
there has been an emergency due to the storm.

And the emergency is a tree which has fallen on
the roof of Uncle Ted and JoJo's apartment and
now for their own complete safety they are NOT
allowed to be there having Christmas for two.

And, just like Marcie said she would,
Granny has a good idea.

And this is it:

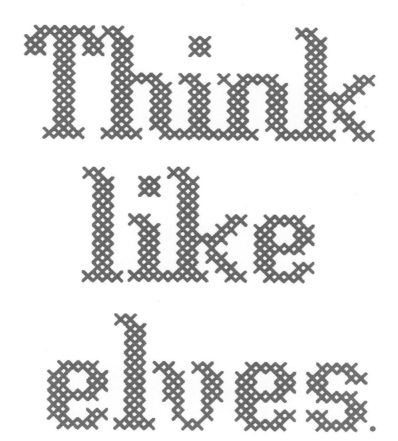

So that's what we decide to do:

Clean up.

Set the table.

Make dinner.

And most of all say **sorry**.

And then we all get cleaning.

And when we have finished cleaning we set the table.

By the time we have finished you would
think the elves had been over.

We are very pleased with ourselves until Marcie
says, "But what about dinner?"

Everybody is a BLANK because nobody knows
what the answer is. Then Grandad comes in
through the front door with Cement.
They are very *windblown* with their hair off
in the wrong direction.

Grandad says, "We just bumped into our friend Karl
and he gave us this envelope—it's for you, Clarice."

It is all decorated in Christmas stickers and it says
in Karl's writing: **Open now or save until later.**

So I open now. Inside there is a very neatly written-out recipe and a note from Karl that says:

Mrs. Tomassini taught me how to make this dinner and I bet you could make it too! Merry Christmas, Clarice Bean

from Karl

PS it is really good

One thing I'm sure about is that we do have the main ingredient. And now I utterly know what to make for dinner.

At seventeen minutes past six, Mom comes
home with Dad, who has arrived back with
NO presents but, instead, Uncle Ted and JoJo.
They all look very tired.
   But they perk up when Uncle Ted says,
      "What's cooking?"

and JoJo says, "Oh wow, that smells so amazing."

Mom says, "Is that *dinner*?"

and Minal says, "It's macaroni!"

and I say, "And cheese."

Dad says, "Did the elves visit while we were gone?"

and Mom says, "I don't remember the house EVER being this clean,"

and JoJo says, "You've gone MINIMALIST."

Mom says, "Yes, where's ALL the clutter?"

and Marcie says, "We put it in the shed."

Grandad says, "Where's my puzzle?"

Minal says, "I vacuumed it up!"

and Kurt says,

"Dinner is served."

And then we all sit down, and I spoon out the macaroni and cheese, which everybody agrees is exceptionOrdinarily better than any other kind of macaroni and cheese because it has a twist and the twist is vegetables.

JoJo says, "I can't believe you cooked this yourselves."

Marcie says, "It was mostly Clarice."

I say, "Everyone helped."

Mom says, "I'm so glad you found a USE for ALL that macaroni," and Dad says, "Yes, who knew you could actually eat it?"

Uncle Ted says, "I hope lunch tomorrow will be this delicious."

Mom says, "Ah yes, that's the GOOD news: Ted and JoJo will be staying for Christmas," and JoJo says, "It's SO generous of you to share your Christmas with US."

Mom: "But of course—

that's what Christmas is about."

Dad: "And we have plenty to share. I accidentally ordered a much-too-big turkey."

Mom: "Ah, that's the BAD news."

Dad: "What do you mean the BAD news?"

And I say,

"The bad news is *my* fault because you told me
NOT to put it in the kitchen fridge
or there would be chaos
and there WAS chaos."

Dad: "Could someone explain?"

Kurt: "It was all my fault for not putting it in the shed like you asked."

Dad: "Are we talking turkey?"

Marcie: "It's probably Cement's fault—
he's the one who ate it."

Uncle Ted: "Cement ate the turkey?"

Minal: "And was sick on the floor."

Grandad: "Oh, dear—it's probably my fault for allowing Cement to eat from the table."

Marcie: "Cement wasn't eating from the table."

Grandad: "He opened the fridge?"

Minal: "The fox ate most of it."

JoJo: "You have a fox?"

Grandad: "I'm confused."

Mom: "Minal, would you please STOP talking about the imaginary fox!"
and I say, "Sorry, because it was
actually ALL my fault,"
and Kurt says,
"Sorry, because it was also MY fault,"
and Grandad says,
"Sorry, because Cement should know better than to eat turkeys dropped on the floor," and Mom says, "Never mind."

Dad says, "If a missing turkey can have everyone in such agreement, then I am glad Cement ate it . . . I wish he hadn't been sick on the floor, but it's a SMALL price to pay for a happy household."

Even without the Advent candle you can tell it is going to be Christmas Day tomorrow because the Christmas spirit has utterly returned and it is interesting that everyone has gone back to being more like their Christmas selves now that we are nine. It is beginning to feel a lot like Christmas.

Mom gets up and peers into the pantry. She says, "I wonder what we will eat tomorrow?" and Dad says, "Something potatoey, I think."

I say, "It's a shame Marguerite isn't coming.
She is a very inventive cook."

We listen to the wind whistling around the
house and the tree tapping at the window, and
Mom says, "I do hope they all arrived safely at the
Robertses'—it's not nice weather to be driving in."

Dad says, "Nine hours is a long time to be in a car."

Grandad says, "It's very chilly out.
I hope they've taken their warm socks."

Mom looks distracted and says,
"Where are Ted and JoJo going to sleep?"

Kurt says, "They can have my room—I can
sleep on the floor of the TINY study,"
and everyone smiles.

Except for Dad, who goes to fetch the yellow
rubber gloves and the air freshener.

My brother's room is a danger to germs.

★ ★ ★

While everyone is moving things from one place
to another and freshening up Kurt's bedroom,
I go and finish working on my Christmas presents.

Luckily, I have made so much fudge there is plenty for Uncle Ted and JoJo with quite a lot left over for emergencies. Once I have put it into the paper heart decorations and attached my gift tags, I hang them all on the tree. Grandad says it looks very eye-catching and I think I agree. This is the successful part and so long as no one tries to eat it, it will be a good present.

After everything has been completely done, we all sit down to watch the film of Mary Poppins. Even Kurt watches and no one complains at all. Then we put our stockings on the end of our beds and turn out the light and try our best to go to sleep even though some of us are still chatting downstairs and keeping other people awake.

It is hard to go to sleep because how can you get your heart to stop beating so much and your mind to stop wishing for the morning? And the more you want to sleep, the more you can't. I am almost on the very edge of *drifting* off when I seem to hear a piano, and my ears stand up on end and I wait and I think I am definitely listening to tuneful notes.

And so I tiptoe downstairs
in the absolute dark.
And only the Christmas tree
lights are awake.

And I peek into the living room and my eyes
adjust to the twinkling gloom,
and next to the fireplace there are the eaten-up
gingerbread crumbs and the milk's ALL
gone. And this can only mean you-know-who has
been down the chimney.
  So I quietly creep back up to my bed and I
listen to the storm and think about how the
wind *blows* Mary Poppins to the door.

And I wish it could do the same for us—
    I wish the wind could *blow*
        more people to *our* door.

And I wish it could bring the snow.
    I wish it could.

        And just before I fall
            into my dreams . . .

I am sure I can hear the sound
of whispering elves
playing a piano.

TWELVE

Have Yourself a Merry Little Christmas

I WAKE UP AND WE ALL WAKE UP, AND this is what happens.

With my toes I can feel something heavy on the end of my bed and right away I know two things.

ONE: Santa and the elves have definitely been here.

TWO: There is NOT a piano in my stocking.

My eyes are only slightly adjusted to the morning, since it is 6:22 on the alarm clock, and so it takes me a few milliseconds to realize that my bedroom is FULL of cousins. Yolla and Noah are standing there readily dressed for Christmas in their Christmas presents. I am astonished of course.

Minal says, "How are you here when you are at the Robertses'?"

and Noah says, "Because we didn't GO,"

and Yolla says, "NO, we aren't there."

We all open my stocking and even though there isn't even one thing from on my list, I can see that actually Santa has had some good ideas of his own.

For instance, e.g., a TINY tape-measure key ring, which I know for a fact he got from the post-office-convenient store—it still has the price tag on it.

So I suppose it DOES make sense that he buys his wrapping paper from there too.

We all go down for breakfast, where most people are eating eggs in pajamas.

Marguerite says, "You see, Clarice Bean, your wish came true!"

I say, "Oh, did the Robertses get infectious stomach bugs?"

Al says, "Not as far as I know. The problem is our car—it's

suffering from old age. It wouldn't start because the weather's too cold," and Marguerite says, "I didn't like the look of the weather at all—it's getting icy."

They all look really pleased.

Mom says, "Just imagine if it had snowed and you'd gotten stuck in the middle of nowhere?"

And then *I* look really pleased.

Dad says, "It's not going to snow."

Minal ate too many jellybeans and has started running around and around the kitchen, so Mom puts a hat on him and makes him run around and around the yard twenty-seven times. It's quite funny to watch and Noah takes several pictures with his instant camera, which came in his stocking.

Al says that Noah and Yolla opened ALL their presents

at five o'clock in the morning, and this makes me think about Grandad because he is usually an early riser, so where is he?

Uncle Ted says, "He's popped over to Peggy's to wish her and her family a merry Christmas."

Mom says, "She is going to be so busy. There are thirteen of them, you know."

I say, "The same as us." Since with the added cousins and uncle and aunt we are now thirteen.

Dad says, "Lucky for some."

Once we've had breakfast, Mom starts rummaging in the pantry to see what we can have for Christmas dinner now that the main part of it has been eaten by a dog. We are all adapting to a vegetable-only lunch and probably spaghetti when Grandad comes home with Peggy.

Mom says, "Peggy! We are so happy to see you!" and Marguerite says, "Is your family outside?" and Peggy says, "It's a long story!"

Which actually it isn't because they are just stuck at abroad airports due to stormy conditions and the planes not being allowed up. So no one at all is coming until at least tomorrow.

Dad says, "Will you join us for spaghetti and brussels sprouts?" and Peggy says, "Close your eyes and make a wish."

And when we open them there is a

HUGE turkey
on the table.

Peggy says, "Merry Christmas, one and all!"

Noah says, "Where did THAT come from?" and Peggy says, "My kitchen."

Dad says, "You didn't *carry* it all the way here, did you?" and Peggy says, "No, I used an old shopping cart that was parked outside my house." She says, "It was like an angel left it there for just this very reason."

And now, just like that, we are fourteen. It means lunch will become dinner because GIANT turkeys take a lot of time to cook, and Dad says it might be a good idea if some of us go for a run around. He is mainly looking at Minal, who is still very hyperly-active from the jellybeans.

So most of us go for a walk up the hill,
and we meet Karl and Alf, who is feeling better,
and we climb up the trees,
and we *race* around the woods,
and we are gone forever even though it is cold
and we almost turn blue in the toes
and no one wants to STOP.
But in the end we have to,
so we say goodbye to Karl and Alf
and walk back
down
the
hill.

When we turn the corner
   we see Dad is waiting
at the end of our street,
   wondering
      where
         we are.

By the time we get home everyone
is really quite exceptionordinarily
hungry and nearly frozen to ice.

Mom has lit all the candles
and the house looks like one of those
old-fashioned paintings
from the past.

We all sit down and we are just about
to start eating when Peggy says,
"Do you hear that?"
   And Mom says, "Yes, I think I do."
   Minal says, "Is it a FOX?"
   JoJo says, "I think it's singing."
   Yolla says, "A singing fox?"
   Marcie says, "Carol singers."
   Kurt says, "Where is it coming from?"
   Uncle Ted says, "Outside the door,"
and Dad says,
   "Clarice, go take a look."

And so I do.

It is already dark, but I can see four people
and a dog standing on the doorstep singing,
and the song is
"We Wish You a Merry Christmas"
and the dog is Pekingese and it is wearing
a choirboy costume.

And the amazing thing is it's all of the
Moodys on our actual doorstep.
And they all say,

"Merry Christmas, Clarice Bean!"

I say, "How are you here when you are on the
plane to Japan?"
And Betty says, "Your mom called us
because she thought we might be stuck at
the airport due to wind."
Call-me-Mol says, "I hope you don't mind us
bringing Ralph? We borrowed him back
from the neighbors."
Grandad says, "Cement will be pleased."

And now, just like that, we are nineteen if you
count Ralph, but since he is dressed as a boy I do.

It is a Squash . . .

but we all squish around the table
and everyone fits exactly.

★ ★ ★

After dinner I give out my fudge, which is enough
for one each and Peggy says it is more like old-
fashioned toffee, and toffee in her opinion is nicer
than fudge, even if you do have to chop it up with
a hammer. Minal is NOT allowed to eat his until
tomorrow in case it sets him off again because,
you see, there is not enough room to have a boy
running around the kitchen.

Betty is very pleased with the **RUBY REDFORT
FLY LIGHT** and it is passed around the room
and Grandad says he will put it on his Christmas
list for next year.

And *everyone* is very pleased with all their
presents—*including* me—and so I am utterly
surprised when Mom says,

"Oh, we almost forgot; Santa left

THIS one here last night—it's for YOU."

And Uncle Ted jumps up, and Dad jumps up,
and they slowly *DRAG* the Christmas tree
away from the wall until I can see a large shape
through the branches.

Dad says, "I guess it wouldn't **squeeze** into a stocking."

And I realize Betty Moody was right.
I have NOT been believing in NOTHING
after all—I just needed to use a stamp.
    And I say,
        "I *knew* I could hear the elves
                playing the piano last night."
    And Betty whispers, "You see, Clarice Bean,
you didn't even need a backup plan."
    Call-me-Cecil sits down on the little stool
and says, "So what shall we sing?"
and I say, "How about 'Let it Snow'?"
    And we sing and sing
and everyone stays up very, very late
without getting tired and we play charades
and the drawing game and cards
until it is time for the Moodys and Peggy and
the cousins to leave and although we are sorry
to see them go, when we open the door
    to wave goodbye to them,
                you will not believe it
        because it is the kind of thing
                which only happens in books
                        or in the movies.

Because, you see . . .

it is   really utterly snowing.

The End of Things

WE CALLED GRANNY VERY LATE ON
Christmas night to tell her that it had been
quite an unexpected day of exactly
what it was supposed to be.

And even though there were 114 potatoes
to peel, nobody flumped in a chair with
tiredness and that's because nineteen people,
which includes a choirboy dog,
is always the right number
for Christmas.

Granny said she was very pleased with all the
old sweaters. It is NOT what she was expecting
and she has a feeling that it is NOT what Mom
had expected to be sending her, but it couldn't be
more suitable, because she and her friend Wallace

are planning to do some mending and
set up a stall selling reconditioned knitwear.
She said she will mend my cardigans
and send them right back to me.

Mom looked at me and said,
"I wonder what Mr. Felixstow is thinking
about his unexpected delivery." She explained to
Granny about the mix-up and Granny said,
"I am sure he will be very comfortable in
my new slippers, but the prescription sunglasses
may give him eye-ache."

Mom said, "He must think we've gone a bit loopy.
What's he going to do with ALL those
peculiar presents?"

Dad said, "He can always cook the macaroni necklace."

And Grandad said, "I think Mr. Felixstow will wonder how he ever managed without a TINY-USEFUL-THINGS BAG."

And Granny said, "Exactly."

I told her I would make her another one and she said she would look forward to it and she hoped the **RUBY REDFORT LONG-DISTANCE WALKIE-TALKIES** might arrive in time for my birthday.

And I said I would look forward to that and then we all said goodbye.

And now it is time to go up to bed and even though I don't want it to be over, my eyes are beginning to fall asleep without me.

But while I am slowly climbing the stairs, I think about the day and even though I didn't get the fish or the tank it doesn't matter, because I can put them on my list for next Christmas.

Minal gave me the fish food, which was really very thoughtful, and it doesn't expire for another six years, so I have plenty of time.

Just before I climb into bed, I tiptoe over to the window and look out at the snowflakes falling, and I can hear Uncle Ted playing the piano and he is singing a song about the snow and the words carry me away and remind me of my Advent-candle wish and how it came true— and it's just like Ruby Redfort says,

"How can your wishes come TRUE, if you NEVER even bother to wish?"

Then I tuck myself into bed,
close my eyes,
and
drift
into
dreams.

"Oh my goodness, there's a fox in the kitchen."

"I told you there was!"

Christmas songs adapted by Clarice Bean

**Christmas Is Coming,
the Goose Is Getting Fat**
"Christmas Is Coming"
traditional nursery rhyme and song, first set to music in 1800s

**Goodwill
to All Peoplekind**
"It Came Upon a Midnight Clear"
based on the poem by Edmund Sears, 1849

Glad Tidings of Great Joy
"While Shepherds Watched Their Flocks"
traditional carol from around 1700

Hark How the Bells
"Carol of the Bells"
lyrics by Mykola Leontovych and
music by Peter Wilhousky, 1914

Joy to the World
"Joy to the World"
by Isaac Watts, 1719

Merrily on High
"Ding Dong Merrily on High"
by George Ratcliffe Woodward, 1924

**Christmas Tree,
O Christmas Tree**
"O Christmas Tree"
traditional 16th century
German carol, lyrics 1824

**Deck the Halls
with Boughs of Holly**
"Deck the Halls"
traditional 16th century carol,
lyrics by Thomas Oliphant, 1862

Sing Choirs of Angels
"O Come All Ye Faithful"
traditional carol from around 1744

In the Bleak Midwinter
"In the Bleak Midwinter"
based on the poem by Christina Rossetti, 1872

**It's Beginning to Look
a Lot Like Christmas**
"It's Beginning to Look a Lot Like Christmas"
by Meredith Wilson, 1951

**Have Yourself a Merry
Little Christmas**
"Have Yourself a Merry Little Christmas"
by Hugh Martin and Ralph Blane, 1943

More exceptionOrdinarily good books
by Lauren Child

THE CLARICE BEAN NOVELS:

Utterly Me,
Clarice Bean

Clarice Bean
Spells Trouble

Clarice Bean,
Don't Look Now

THE CLARICE BEAN PICTURE BOOKS:

Clarice Bean,
That's Me

Clarice Bean,
Guess Who's Babysitting?

THE RUBY REDFORT SERIES:

RUBY REDFORT *LOOK INTO MY EYES*

RUBY REDFORT *TAKE YOUR LAST BREATH*

RUBY REDFORT *CATCH YOUR DEATH*

RUBY REDFORT *FEEL THE FEAR*

RUBY REDFORT *PICK YOUR POISON*

RUBY REDFORT *BLINK AND YOU DIE*

I would like to thank the following for all their
talent, support, and inspiration:

**Rachel Folder, Goldy Broad, Lydia Barram, Sam Stewart,
Val Brathwaite, KB, and David Mackintosh.**

**Tuesday Child for the Advent calendar drawing
and for baking the lemon drizzle cake.**

**Mini Steward for writing the numbers and
Bibi Steward for making the paper heart basket.**

**Special thanks as always to AJM,
and of course to AD for his unerring support.**

This is a
work of fiction. Names, characters,
places, and incidents are either products
of the author's imagination or, if real, are used fictitiously.

Copyright © 2021 by Lauren Child

First US edition 2022
First published by HarperCollins (UK) 2021

Library of Congress Catalog Card Number 2021953117
ISBN 978-1-5362-2365-1

22 23 24 25 26 27 TTP 10 9 8 7 6 5 4 3 2 1

Printed in Huizhou, Guangdong, China

This book was typeset in Bembo.

Candlewick Press
99 Dover Street
Somerville, Massachusetts 02144

www.candlewick.com

Thanks to Hachette Children's Books for use of the Clarice Bean series lettering